PATRICK'S RUN

Patrick's Run

Written and published by
James A. McQuiston, FSA Scot
jamesamcquiston@gmail.com

Printed in the U.S.A.
All Rights Reserved
©2017

This publication is designed to provide accurate information, in the form of historical fiction, concerning a man who sacrificed for his country and died a horrible death. Every effort has been made to accurately combine official military documents, the historical records of many locations, and the author's own knowledge of events and places involved in this story. The author and publisher accepts no liability for any harm alleged to be caused based on the contents of this book. *Patrick's Run* is meant only to tell the best possible story of this unsung American hero.

The author can be contacted at: jamesamcquiston@gmail.com

*Lo! He fought so brave at Erie,
Freely served, and nobly dared,
Let his courage plead for mercy,
Let his precious life be spared.*

Table of Contents

- 7 *Preface*
- 11 *Chapter One:* The Harvest
- 23 *Chapter Two:* Presqu' Isle
- 33 *Chapter Three:* Up Lake
- 43 *Chapter Four:* The Battle Engaged
- 53 *Chapter Five:* The Aftermath
- 63 *Chapter Six:* The News Arrives
- 73 *Chapter Seven:* A New Life
- 85 *Chapter Eight:* The Crime
- 97 *Chapter Nine:* The Trial
- 111 *Chapter Ten:* The Execution
- 119 *Chapter Eleven:* The Response
- 127 *Epilogue*

Preface

The story presented in this book can be found nowhere else. It was written after a large amount of investigation, and is made available here for the very first time.

Some of the tale you are about to read is based on known facts, some on logical conjecture, and some is fictionalized or dramatized. The goal is to create an interesting book, which, at the same time, gives credit to a great man.

Over two hundred years ago, an aging Irish immigrant risked his life for America. In return, he went deaf in battle. In return, he found himself stranded in a small frontier town, unable to contact what little family he had left. In return, he found himself the victim of misplaced justice. And, in return, he was hanged an innocent man, a forgotten man, an unsung American hero.

But not unsung anymore.

Chapter One
THE HARVEST

Patrick Fitzpatrick held onto the wheel of his hay wagon in the hot, early August sun. He gasped for fresh air, but smelled only the manure of his draft horse, and the heaviness of hay seeds floating in the sunlight.

It had been dry now for three days straight. Dry and hot. Now was the time he'd waited for – time to harvest his first crop of cut grass, on his very first farm.

It was odd that a fifty-five-year-old seafarer would just now be getting around to farming in the northwest Pennsylvania wilderness.

His son Hugh had given up on the lake back in 1810, and settled along a little creek that he called Hugh's Run.

It took Patrick another three years to leave the body of water they called Lake Erie, and to locate his own farm on another creek, which he named Patrick's Run.

Little did he know that, 200 years later, this creek would still be called "Patrick Run," though no one then would remember him.

The Harvest

But it was a different body of water that he thought about on this hot summer's day.

The *Eriez* Indian name translates as "Cat Nation," based on the legend that Lake Erie held an underwater panther who mostly lay quiet, until suddenly springing up, usually during a storm, to attack unsuspecting sailors and fishermen.

Patrick had learned to read the "Cat." He was, in fact, considered the best pilot on the lake. But so much had happened recently that caused him to reconsider his life.

There was the tragedy that took place when Judah Colt sent three men to Freeport with a load of supplies for his station, back in '97 or '98. All three drowned when the Cat decided to pounce. That was sad enough, but not as sad as when three young boys, all sons of war widows, went out too early in the spring to fish. A fourth stayed behind because of his own widowed mother's fears.

And she was right to fear.

Fishing out of Freeport, along the Pennsylvania shoreline, the boys saw that the spring weather that year was calm, and that the ice had cleared over most of the lake. It was only a few weeks ago that they heard it crack. Then the winds blew. Then the ice melted, except along the bluffs.

The three loaded up their gang of nets and headed out. Before they knew it, they were out of sight of land when a fierce storm blew up. When they hadn't returned by nightfall, fires were lit along the shoreline to help guide them in. Morning came with no boys in sight. A rescue boat was launched as soon as the water calmed. A gang of nets was found about two miles out. A few days later, wreckage from the boat washed up further east, on a small beach.

But the boys? They were never found.

Little did these victims know they would be among just the first few casualties of this lake, bound and determined as she was to eventually take thousands of souls to her depths, with hundreds of sailing vessels lost in storms, and a lake bottom littered with debris, immigrant trunks, and a fair amount of treasure likely never to be recovered.

The deaths of the three supply men, followed later by the deaths of the three young fishermen, sent a chill through navigators of this shallowest of Great Lakes.

The final straw for Patrick happened one day as he sailed alone in a small skiff to check on a stranded supply raft. All was well, with a west wind gently driving his sail forward.

Then suddenly, and literally out of the blue, a gust directly from the north forced his sail over his head, the boom scuffing his scalp, nearly knocking him senseless. It was all he could do to straighten the boat, rudder in one hand, lowering the sail with the other, his head burning with pain.

Though an old hand at sailing, and on this lake in particular, this event took him by surprise, and he suffered from headaches for many weeks after, until he finally decided enough was enough.

This potentially fatal event proved convincing enough for Patrick Fitzpatrick to decide now would be a good time to join his son in the nearly unpopulated land just south of the old French settlement of Presqu' Isle, reclaimed by the British, and now by Americans.

Away from the lake, land was cheap, nearly free.

Besides, Master Commander Perry was building a small fleet in the bay at Presqu' Isle to face off soon against the British who were anchored just off the Canadian shore. Perry needed supplies, including hay for horses and cattle. And so, Patrick thought it much safer to be away from the conflict, but still be able to profit a bit from it.

Despite his suffering from "summer catarrh," caused by the polluted air about him (later to be known as hay fever), Patrick had his reddened eyes set on a bigger prize, that of selling wagon loads of straw to Perry's men. He expected them to come by his farm soon.

Someone had been asking about him recently. He was told this by his own son. Could it be they heard of his seventy-five acres of hay fields?

"Seventy-five acres!" he thought, "How will I ever get through all this hay?"

His body showed the tell-tale signs of a farmer's tan. His forearms were reddish brown, up to the edge of his rolled-up sleeves. His neck was blood red.

A wet rag did its best to beat back the heat during the haying process, but still he suffered from the unfamiliar foulness of the air, and the relentless rays of the sun.

He remembered back to his days on the lake when he would often work a gang of whitefish nets, shirtless, with pant legs rolled up, and bare feet.

He was strong back then, strong and brown, with lungs full of fresh breezes – breezes that kept him cool and exhilarated.

But war and near tragedy had led him down a new path. It was also a joy to be within walking distance of his sons, and it was only fair to his wife, Honora Mary Madigan Fitzpatrick, as fine a woman as County Clare, Ireland ever produced, who had spent so many of her days in a widow's watch, waiting for his return.

"Ah, Mary," he thought. "You passed so soon, leaving Lil' Patrick behind, and just as we bought our own farm."

Hugh was now raising his younger brother, Lil' Patrick, while their father learned the ways of the field.

"Mary," the old man continued, "I know you believed I loved the lake more than you. It's true, she had a hold of me. The challenge, the mystery, that fickle Cat. But it was you I truly loved since we first met in County Clare, near the Shannon. Ya should've known then that the open water called to me. I should've known myself."

He remembered his own father's fishing boat flipping over in a gale, with its owner lashed to the mast. When the storm ceased, the eastward winds brought the dead man home. Why didn't he see then that this was no life?

"Mr. Fitzpatrick!"

Startled, Patrick turned to see a gallant figure astride an equally gallant horse, silhouetted in the sun.

"Who are you?" he said, as he moved for the rifle leaning against the wagon.

Patrick always kept a flintlock with him to fend off bears and wildcats, or, if he was lucky, to bring game meat home for supper.

"No need for that," the rider spoke. "I'm your friend, Richard Smith – Colonel Richard Smith, if you please."

"Smithy! Jesus, Joseph and Mary! Get down off that horse and give me a hug."

The two men embraced quickly, sharing a link that could never be broken, a link built while facing danger together, while drinking to the tune of a fiddle until morning, and while swapping deep secrets.

"For the life of me I didn't recognize you in that get up. Maybe it was the sun," Patrick guessed, looking for an excuse for his own lack of cognition.

"This? This is no get up my friend. This is what I will wear as I go into battle against the British."

"Battle against the British? Again? Hadn't we had enough of that in our twenties? Guess not."

"Yes, I guess not; at least for me. The question is – What about you?"

"What about me?"

"Yes – What about you?"

Patrick stood silent for a moment or two. Then it dawned on him – "Oh no ya don't. You're not gettin' me back in a uniform. I can barely ride a horse anyway, with all my aches and pains."

"There won't be any horse riding."

"What do you mean?"

"I mean the only thing you'll be riding is a wave on Lake Erie."

"A wave, ya say? And where'd I be goin'?"

"You'll be going to Put-in-Bay, leading the charge against the British fleet."

"Me?"

"Yes, you. I told Perry that you are the best man to lead us there, and lead us there by next month."

Patrick had been to Put-in-Bay often. Since the late 1700s, this was one of the few places schooners and fishing boats could wait out a storm, if they were lucky enough to be on the west end of the lake. The not-so-lucky ones, especially over to the east, at Long Point, or down by Freeport, were often run aground, split up, broken deep to take on water, or capsized helplessly in the grip of the Cat.

"Well, first of all, that yankee Perry knows nothing about sailing on rough water."

Smith objected, "Why he's been all over the world's oceans. Even the Mediterranean Sea."

"Mediterranean or not, he's never seriously sailed on a body of water like Lake Erie – a hissing panther just waitin' to drag you into her lair."

"And that, my good friend, is why I am here. You have sailed on Lake Erie. You are the best this country has at it. We need you, and we need you now."

"Just hold on a damn minute, here. I'm not gonna give up this farm I just spent my life savings on, leave my poor wife's grave, and walk away from my sons, livin' just down the road from here. I've got seventy-five acres here, and a nice little creek that I call Patrick's Run."

Patrick walked quickly over to a little trickle of water.

"It isn't much now, but in the springtime she'll run a small mill wheel, or float a small log. Right now, you could spit in it and flood the place."

"You and your sons won't be living here long if the British have their way. They've stirred up the tribes in the Ohio Valley, led by Tecumseh. If he and his braves get their hands on you, that nice old head of hair will be gracing one of their spears, as they head east to the next settlement."

"That bad, huh?"

"That bad."

"Smithy, I gotta think about this a little. I gotta talk to Hugh, and consider my youngest, Lil' Patrick."

As an afterthought, he asked, "What about my hay? I've been workin' and waitin' all summer for this crop. I'm not gonna waste it."

"Commander Perry will be more than happy to pay you top dollar for your hay, and top dollar for your services on a sloop leading the charge."

"When do I need to be there?"

"Some of the ships have already left for Saundustee. We prepare to sail with the balance of them on the second day of September."

Patrick thought for a moment.

"I'll be there then, with my load of hay, too."

Smithy looked at Patrick. "You know, old man, I love you like my brother. I wouldn't ask this of you if I didn't think it was the only way."

"Smithy, I can't bring myself to thank you! – especially now that you got me in this pickle. But I'll be there. Don't you worry. We'll run them British home just like we did the last time."

At right – Patrick's Run is clearly shown "running" into Clear Lake near Spartansburg, Pennsylvania, located just south of Lake Erie. This creek is now known simply as "Patrick Run," and few know the real story behind it's name. Patrick Fitzpatrick's land would have bordered this creek, or perhaps surrounded it completely.

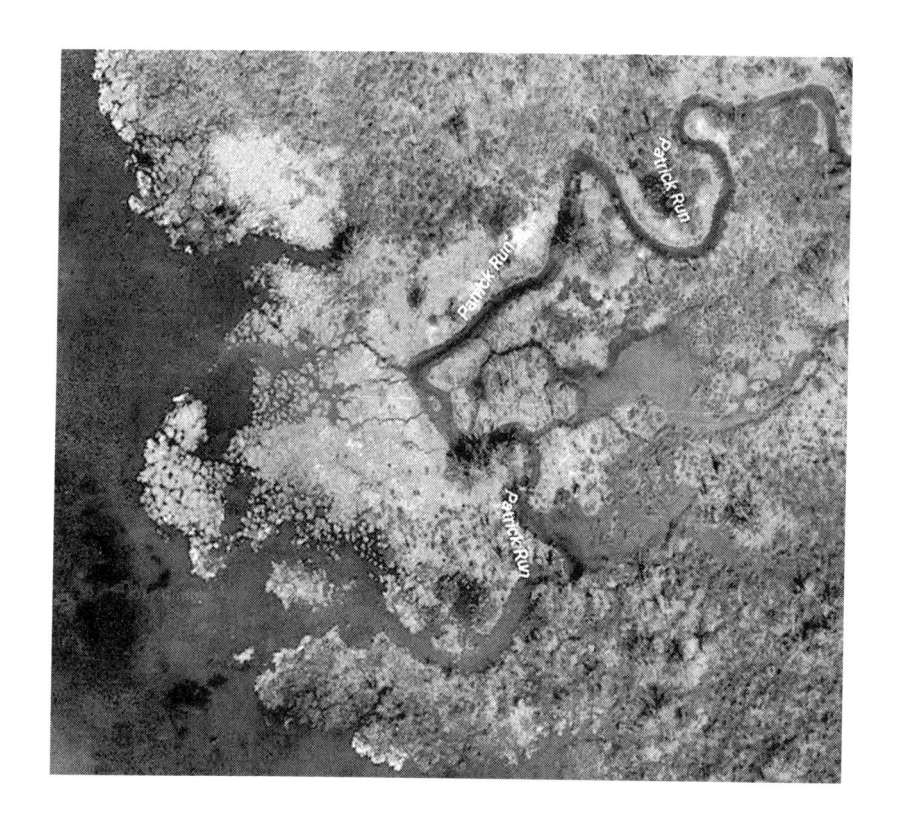

Patrick's Run

Chapter Two
Presqu' Isle

The lake shore always held the heat better than land located just over the ridge that separated it from Patrick's Run. Even though it was only the first day of September, Patrick could feel the difference. Back on the farm, the hot summer days of August had just barely given way to fall winds, but here, on the shores of the Cat, on the shores of Lake Erie, the sun still shone bright, the water still reflected warmth all around.

Patrick knew, and he'd told so many folks, that this warmer shoreline would someday be covered with orchards – apples, grapes, berries and more. It was only a matter of time, what with all the new settlers moving in, slowed only by the threat of war.

He mused, "All these Jack tars and infantry will see how beautiful the sunsets are here, and want to bring their families. Blue water is many days away for most folks. Yep. It's only a matter of time."

"I got a load of hay, here, for Perry," he said, to the first soldier he saw at Presqu' Isle.

"Wait your turn, old man."

"Old man?" replied the fifty-five-year-old Patrick,

as he threatened to swing at the jaw of this young upstart. But his hand was stopped by an even stronger hand.

"Patrick, when are you going to learn?" came a voice from behind. It was Smithy, with a big smile on his face.

"How many times have I told you – you don't need to solve every problem with your fist? Besides, we've got enough other folks out there to do battle with. Sergeant Wilkins, take this man's wagon to the front of the line and see that he gets paid well for his hay."

"Yes, sir!"

"Well, I guess you got some pull around here after all. Just don't think you'll be tellin' me when and when not to use my fists."

"Patrick. You crazy old goat."

The two friends walked to a nearby log structure – one of the few real buildings in this rough little settlement of Erie.

Smithy introduced Patrick to the keeper of the establishment. "This here's John Dickson."

"Hell! I know who John Dickson is."

Turning to the innkeeper, he said, "You been here since '08, right?"

"That's right, Patrick, and once this nasty war gets over I'm gonna build me a real public house, maybe two or three stories tall. Thinking 'bout getting Bill Himrod to do the construction. But this ain't gonna be no ordinary Dickson's Tavern. Nope, nothing like that. I'm gonna name it the Exchange Coffee House."

"The what?" Patrick exclaimed.

"The Exchange Coffee House. I'm gonna cater to all the high-class folks that are going to rush into this city."

"Hmm, you see it like I do. There's no way on God's green earth that this place isn't gonna prosper. Think about it. There's no other seaport less than a month or more travel east. Plus you can go west from here. Someday, even little crossroads like Detroit will be booming. Too many people. Too few places to go. Especially ones this beautiful."

"Well then, we are in agreement. This calls for an ale," Dickson replied.

"No ale for me," objected Col. Smith. "I have work to do to get these ships ready to sail."

"No ale for me either," spoke up Patrick. "I'll take a bottle of whiskey."

"Patrick!" Smithy warned, "We'll be sailing soon. You need to be ready, with a clear mind."

"You're right. And there's nothin' like a sip of whiskey to clear the mind. I'll catch up with you soon."

As evening came upon the small, busy settlement Patrick found himself on a bluff overlooking the lake, a half-empty bottle of whiskey in his hand. "She's a beauty," he thought, "Sun settin' low through the clouds, all sparklin' red and pink, like some angel weepin'. She ain't no angel, though," he continued to mused, "She's a cat, a ruthless, sneaky cat ready to take her prey down. But ain't she pretty? She is such an angel."

With that, Patrick Fitzpatrick, began to fall asleep in the loamy sand of a Lake Erie bluff.

"Patrick!"

"There's that voice again," he thought.

"Patrick, you're not sleeping out here in the cold and damp."

"Well, I ain't sleeping in no tight quarters on the lower deck o' one of them ships out there, either."

"No you're not. I have a nice warm, dry tent waiting for you, with a nice soft cot."

"Nice soft cot? Who are you tryin' to fool?" Patrick demanded, "I'll sleep on the floor like I always do."

As the two friends walked toward the military encampment, Col. Smith pointed to a dimly-lit boat out in the bay.

"See that sloop over there? That's the one you'll be piloting."

"I see her a little, but what's that confounded noise?"

"Oh, the camels?"

"Camels?"

"Patrick, did you not wonder how we got such big beautiful boats out of the bay?"

"Well, my mind's been on farming as of late. Never thought about it."

"See the men at the bar working those large pumps? They are pumping the last bit of water out of those giant pontoons to get them out of the water lest a victorious British fleet should use them to gain access to Presqu' Isle Bay."

Col. Smith further explained that the so-called "camels" were pontoons filled with water that were then attached to the hulls of the larger ships. As the water was pumped out, the ship would rise just enough to clear the bar at the mouth of the bay.

On August 4th, 1813, the flagship *Lawrence* was cameled over the bar. The *Niagara* followed the next day, and just in time, as the British fleet was seen leaving Port Dover, Canada.

A show of force was displayed by Perry, despite no real time to prepare for battle.

This act proved to be enough to cause the British fleet, under Captain Robert Heriot Barclay, to stay away from Presqu' Isle.

This particular day, Barclay decided, was not the day to begin the fight. Little did he know it may well have been his best chance to defeat Perry's fleet.

"That's an amazin' contraption, and an amazin' idea, Smithy," said Patrick.

"My good man, don't credit me, for it was Daniel Dobbins who, having faced this same problem with

Presqu' Isle

ships he's built in this bay, requisitioned the camels. He has overseen the entire operation."

"Did that Dobbins fella build that sloop? What's her name, anyway?"

"She's the United States Sloop *Trippe*, and no, Dobbins did not build her. She was constructed on the Niagara River as a work boat named the *Contractor*. We purchased her last year, and fitted her out for war."

"Where'd the name *Trippe* come from?"

"From the great pirate hunter himself, John Trippe, scourge of the Mediterranean. And like him, we intend to be the scourge of Lake Erie as far as the British are concerned."

"I guess your men are serious about the coming battle then?" Patrick inquired.

"Some are serious. Some are afraid. Some have never even been to sea before, or have only seen light military duty. Rag tag describes a great number of them – rag tag but with hearts filled with the love of freedom. We shall see how they express that love tomorrow, as we head to Put-in-Bay under the best pilot on these waters."

The two men smiled over this remark.

"So tell me – Who's the skipper?"

"The skipper? You mean Oliver Hazard Perry?"

"No. I mean the skipper of that little single-masted sloop I'm supposed to pilot."

"The skipper you inquire about has the unique name of Lieutenant Thomas Holdup Stevens."

"Holdup? Well, I hope he can hold up that sloop long enough for me to get the fleet there and slip away quietly to enjoy my pension."

"I doubt if there'll be any 'slipping away' involved. You'll be needed throughout the battle and hopefully throughout the rout of the British fleet."

"You mean as we run them British back home?"

"Yes, Patrick, as we run them British back home."

At right – This is a drawing of the just recently reconstructed **Trippe** *sloop, originally built in 1813. She was a 60-ton craft carrying 35 crew, with one 24-pound long gun. The 24-pounder was second only to the 36-pounder in firepower, and was a mainstay of many navies across the world, at the time. In 1803, Porter, Barton & Co. of Black Rock (now part of Buffalo, NY) built a sloop named the* **Contractor**, *commanded by Captain William Lee. She was sold to the government in 1812, outfitted for war, and renamed the* **Trippe**. *Piloted by Patrick Fitzpatrick, she was a part of Commodore Perry's fleet, under the command of Lieutenant Thomas Holdup Stevens. The original* **Trippe** *sloop was burned at Buffalo by the British, in December of 1813.*

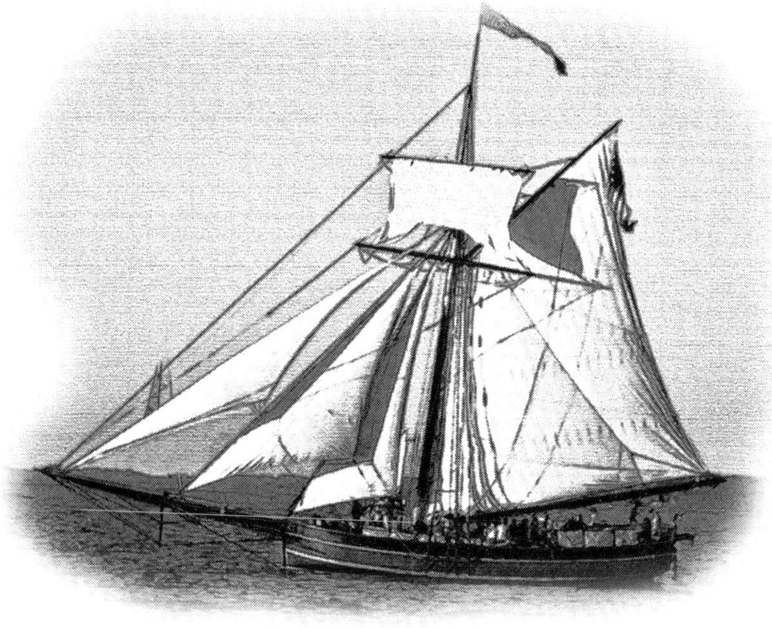

Chapter Three
UP LAKE

The sun was just over the horizon and the morning sky, to the east, was as red as blood – a stark reminder of what might lay ahead.

Patrick noticed a large group of men assembled near the docks. Col. Smith stood on a makeshift platform, facing them. With a toast in his hand, he spoke:

"Lake Erie sing, and make the woods ring, toast your brave heroes, by sea and by land. You Sons of Lake Erie, let us drink to Perry, and toss it about with a full glass in hand."

With that, hats of all types were tossed high, and shouts of "Huzzah" and "Hurrah" rang through the early morning air.

"Poor fools," thought Patrick, "Now they've got to find their hats, while their last minutes on shore, and maybe their last minutes on earth, tick away."

Most of these troops had never been on a ship large enough to sail Lake Erie. The seasoned sailors were already aboard, holding steady until the troops arrived. Most of these troops had never even been in a sea battle. Still, they would show the world that, this fact aside, they weren't about to let the British end the Revolution by winning the War of 1812.

The hectic roar of the battle cry melted into the business of loading arms, ammunition, and men onboard small boats called "tenders," to be transferred out to the larger ships.

Supplies had been loaded already. Many of the now visible weapons were personally owned Pennsylvania and Kentucky long rifles, relics of the Revolution.

They were taken down from fireplaces, or brought out from the back room, cleaned and polished, and made ready to lock and load. Now, with flints taken out to avoid an accidental discharge, they were carried aboard the fleet of Master Commander Oliver Hazard Perry, to once again engage the British.

Patrick had yet to meet the captain of the *Trippe*. He looked around, in vain, for Smithy, through the bustling crowd. "Ah, hell with it," he thought, "I've made it this far in life without a lot of help."

With that, he hollered out, "Any of you brave men headin' to the *Trippe*?"

"Over here," he heard.

"Then I'm goin' with you."

He gingerly climbed aboard and his whole being suddenly filled with energy. "Back on the water again, finally," he thought.

"Here, give me that," he said to one of the oarsmen. The man was more than happy to be relieved of his chore of rowing the tender, and Patrick was more than happy to be propelling himself across the Cat, again.

Once onboard the sloop, Patrick was greeted by a stately man in a very impressive uniform – "Lieutenant Thomas Holdup Stevens, at your service."

Patrick didn't know whether to salute or smile.

"I understand you will be leading the balance of this fleet to Put-in-Bay, as Pilot of this sloop. You must dress the part."

With that, Stevens handed Patrick a pilot's uniform.

"Ah, Captain, you don't expect me to wear that, now do ya?"

"Mr. Fitzpatrick, no officer of mine will be dressed in shoddy civilian clothing. Get below and put this uniform on." He added, "Report to me directly, when you are properly dressed."

"Yes, Sir!" Patrick replied.

As he walked away, he mumbled in his native Gaelic, "*Go n-ithe an Cat thú is go n-ithe an diabhal an Cat* (may the Cat eat you and the devil eat the Cat)!"

"What was that?" Stevens demanded.

"Nothing sir. Just sayin' 'Thank You' in the old tongue."

He hated the idea of a stiff uniform, but it made him feel young again to be in the service, any kind of service, and he was happy to be part of an attack on the British fleet – and right where he felt his best, on the waters of Lake Erie. "Down below" on the *Trippe* was tighter than on other schooners that Patrick had previously sailed on. This sloop was built as a workhorse, with no comforts of home.

He managed to keep his head low as he struggled into the polished uniform of a ship's pilot.

Above, the din of loud voices and the commands necessary to get underway stood in stark contrast to the lonely hay field he'd left just a short while ago, or even to the quiet days he'd spent on this same lake, fishing, piloting crafts for lumber haulers or supply ships, or just sailing across her water for the sheer fun of it.

"As much as I'm glad to be here, right now," he thought, "I'll be twice as happy to be back home to spend winter with my boys."

Patrick Fitzpatrick had no way of knowing, at that moment, that he would never see his farm again. Fate had some terrible days ahead for him. Terrible days.

The slap, slap, slap of water along the hull reminded the old sailor that he had a job to do. He no sooner appeared on deck when Lieutenant Stevens hollered, "Weigh anchor!"

The command was echoed twice across the short deck of the *Trippe*, followed by a series of commands, repeated so that all could hear.

"Mr. Fitzpatrick, to your post!"

"Yes, Sir, Captain!"

Patrick's challenge was not how to lead this fleet to Put-in-Bay. He'd been there enough that he swore he could travel the distance blind-folded.

No. His challenge, that day, was to keep the American naval vessels in line – most new to their crew, and new to Lake Erie.

He was surprised when all the ships fell in nicely behind the *Trippe*. His chest swelled a little to know he was in charge – at least in charge of the voyage up lake.

He headed out far from Presqu' Isle, always watching for deep water, always checking his sextant and the shoreline to the south. This was too important of a job to take any chances.

The fleet soon made its way past the creek where the Massasauga tribe, under Chief Bear's Oil, once took prisoner a young man named Edmund Fitz Jerald, who lived there afterwards for many years. It was just twenty years back that Edmund made a harrowing escape, after much torture and hardship laid upon him by his captors. Patrick wondered if Fitz Jerald was still alive, and harvesting his own hay fields, somewhere over near that shoreline.

"Captain?"

"It's Lieutenant, but yes, Patrick, what is it?"

"Seems to me we've cut old Barclay off from gettin' any supplies at Port Dover. If he comes out of hidin' to make a run for it, do you intend to engage?"

"Yes, Patrick. Very astute of you."

Patrick thought, "Astute? All these 'two-bit' fancy words these officers are using on me are liable to get in the way of some good understanding in the heat of the battle. Best keep my mouth shut, though."

The day wore on until the western isles came into view. Several separate land masses stood in contrast to the east end of the lake where only Presqu' Isle and Long Point dared challenge the Cat.

Patrick had heard, once, that some of these islands had vast cave systems under them, where lake pirates hid treasure. He figured there'd be a lot more pirates to come, once the British were run home.

Yep, the extent of travel on this lake, and the number of associated wrecks, was likely to exceed just about any other place on earth, per square mile.

"Bring us 'round the back side of that larger island, if the channel's deep enough."

"It's deep enough," Patrick assured Stevens.

One by one the tall ships, large and small, edged their way into the calm but deep waters that protected them from dangerous winds. Sails were quickly lowered, anchors dropped overboard, and a few smaller boats lowered to the water to investigate nearby islands.

For the next eight days, nine American ships – a good chunk of the U.S. Navy – awaited their chance to prove themselves.

On entering the war, the Americans had only a dozen ships. Perry added a few more, particularly the *Niagara* and *Lawrence*, both built at Presqu' Isle.

The British sported perhaps the largest navy in the world, with over five hundred warships. Eighty-five of these were roaming the waters around America. But just across Lake Erie, only six were lying in wait to challenge Perry.

Outnumbered nine to six, the British still had more experience fighting at sea, more powerful, longer-range cannons, and ships built with thicker hulls.

It seemed this battle might be won more by seamanship than by firepower or manpower.

If the Americans were victorious, this would hand a blistering and embarrassing defeat to perhaps the world's greatest sea power.

On the eighth day of waiting, on the 10th day of September, the battle commenced.

At right – This list was taken from an article named "The Battle of Lake Erie in Ballad and History," by Charles B. Galbreath, which appeared in 1911. Galbreath was the State Librarian at the State Library of Ohio from 1896–1911. The article appeared in a book by the Ohio State Archaeological and Historical Society, of various archaeological and historical publications. The second name from the bottom clearly shows Patrick Fitzpatrick as a Pilot, receiving $447.39 for his share of the prize money from the Battle of Lake Erie. This would amount to about $5,000 in today's money.

The Battle of Lake Erie in Ballad and History. 451

Names.	Rank.	Amount.	When Paid.
Eli Steward	Quarter-gunner	447 39	July, 1814.
Isaac B. Seal	Pilot	447 39	Dec., 1816.
Godfrey Bowman	Landsman	214 89	July, 1814
Willard Martin	Ordinary seaman	214 89	Dec. 25, 1814.
William Pase	Landsman	214 89	July, 1814.
James Taneyhill	Landsman	214 89	Nov. 11, 1814.
Peter Ozee	Seaman	214 89	July, 1814.
John Smith	Soldier	214 89	Dec. 25, 1814.
Benjamin Hall	Soldier	214 89	July, 1814.
Joseph Wright	Soldier	214 89	Sept 12, 1814.
Hugh Larrimore	Soldier	214 89	Feb. 22, 1815.
E. L. Burting	Soldier	214 89	July, 1814.
Thomas Crossin	Marine	214 89	July, 1815.
Thomas Holdup	Lieut. commandant	2,293 00	July, 1814.
Alexander McCully	Master's mate	1,214 29	July, 1814.
Patrick Fitzpatrick	Pilot	447 39	July, 1814.
John Brown	Boatswain's mate	811 35	Nov. 8, 1814.

Chapter Four
THE BATTLE ENGAGED

The dawn of September 10, 1813, came early.

To the northwest of Put-in-Bay a lookout spotted six British ships advancing just beyond Rattlesnake Island.

The Master Commander of the American fleet began issuing orders and sent a dispatch to the captains of the other ships. It read: "Commanding officers are particularly enjoined to pay attention in preserving their stations in the line, and in all cases to keep as near the *Lawrence* as possible. Engage your designated adversary, in close action, at half cable's length."

The British came to battle with sixty-three cannons, most capable of throwing a forty-two pound ball as far as a mile. Perry, on the other hand, had but fifty-four guns total; just twenty on his flagship, the *Lawrence*.

If America was to win, Perry would have to move his fleet dangerously close to Barclay's, avoiding as much damage to their ships as possible, while hoping for close-quarter action against the enemy.

At 7:00 am, the line of America ships sailed out

The Battle Engaged

from the Put-in-Bay harbor, aiming directly for the six ship flags of the British fleet.

Perry needed to tack west-northwest, due to a west-southwest wind. This was hardly an ideal situation for a fleet intent on closing quarters early in the battle.

Patrick Fitzpatrick did his best to follow.

But, for more than two hours, the American fleet struggled to make headway and, by 10:00 am, Perry made the decision to turn his fleet around.

Just before his order could be implemented, the Cat decided to send her winds southeast, filling American sails with air. After a few quick adjustments, Perry's fleet was finally on the attack course he had planned – to drive forward into close combat as quickly as possible.

Barlcay's fleet continued its forward momentum towards the Americans.

Two American schooners, the *Ariel* and *Scorpion*, were placed off the *Lawrence's* bow to engage the first British vessel. The *Lawrence* was third in line and would engage the *Detroit*, Barclay's 19-gun flagship. Fourth in line, the *Caledonia* was a small brig with only three guns. Fifth came the *Niagara*, Perry's other 20-gun brig, and sister ship to the *Lawrence*.

Fitzpatrick, who a month ago never imagined he'd even be in this situation, was embarrassed, but somewhat pleased to see that the *Trippe*, along with a few of the smaller boats, was forced to hang back, due to less sail-power. They would enter the fray where most needed, as soon as they could catch up.

He noticed, ahead of him, a flag being raised on the *Lawrence*. It seemed to read something like, "Don't Give Up The Ship," as near as he could tell at that distance.

Perry assured his command, just before the battle commenced, "If a victory is to be gained, I will gain it."

His men were filled with the passion that only direct combat could engender. Then they heard it!

It was 11:45, when the *Detroit* unleashed a long-range cannon. The shot landed harmlessly off the bow of the *Lawrence*.

The Americans laughed.

Just minutes later, a second 24-pounder came crashing through the *Lawrence* hull, the wood splinters killing and wounding many men.

The laughing stopped.

The battle was no longer a passionate zeal to teach the British a lesson. It was now a simple matter of survival.

Perry's worst fear of British long guns reaching the thin hulls of the America flagship had just come true.

The *Lawrence* cannons were still out of range, so Perry issued orders to the *Scorpion*, with one long 24-pounder, and the *Ariel*, with four long 12-pounders, to engage.

The Battle Engaged

A half hour went by like an eternity as Perry struggled to close within range.

The *Lawrence* was forced to pass through nearly the entire British line, suffering punishing blows all the way.

Many men, who hadn't even begun to fight, were slain behind the hull they had hoped would protect them, as it shattered into deadly shrapnel.

But, for Perry, there was no other course. He must close with all his ships for his shorter-range guns and his riflemen to have any effect.

For some unknown reason, the *Niagara* seemed to be hesitant to join in the battle. Other smaller sloops, like the *Trippe*, were still struggling to catch up to their larger counterparts.

By 2:30 pm, Perry saw that over half his men lay dying, as the hull of the *Lawrence* continued to shatter.

"Prepare a tender, immediately," he yelled to four nearby crew members.

His purser and chaplain were the only two men of any authority he could readily find, and so he directed them to command the *Lawrence* as it limped away from battle.

Perry quickly lowered his now-famous flag and, draping it over his shoulder, he personally took one last shot at the British fleet with a cannon, then climbed down the Jacob's ladder to the tender below.

Through the hail of British cannon shot, and now even rifle shot, Perry and his men made for the *Niagara*.

As he scaled the rail, Perry quickly commanded, "Double-load the cannons, and engage!"

Just then, the Cat decided to enter the fray once again, as she swung her winds in a favorable direction, allowing Perry's fleet to close fast on his opponents.

Only now arriving on the scene, Patrick headed the *Trippe* directly towards the British fleet, as captain and crew fired furiously. The British returned fire.

Cannon bursts echoed across the sloop, and across the west end of Lake Erie, until the British struck their colors.

Only two men on the *Trippe* were wounded.

The two largest British vessels, the *Detroit* and the *Queen Charlotte*, slammed into each other and locked together.

When the British *Chippeway* and *Little Belt* attempted to flee, the American sloops *Trippe* and *Scorpion* chased them back to their defeated fleet.

Six ship flags of the British were now in the hands of Perry.

Patrick Fitzpatrick suddenly noticed how quiet everything had become. "It's over," he sighed.

The old pilot slumped back against the ship's rail. Something was wrong. Something out of the ordinary. Was he so wounded that he had sunk into delirium?

Lieutenant Stevens knelt beside him to ask, "Patrick? Are you alright? Are you wounded?"

Stevens searched the non-responsive pilot for signs of blood, but found none.

"Patrick! Patrick! Can you hear me?"

Still no response.

Patrick could see that the captain was speaking to him, but he could hear nothing.

Patrick wasn't alone. In his own hurry to attend to his men, Stevens hadn't realized that his own hearing was remarkably muffled and dull.

A fear like nothing Patrick had ever faced spread throughout his being. "This can't be!" he thought.

Fear turned to panic and it was only the strong arms of the lieutenant that kept him still. He cried out, "My ears! What is happening?"

It was then that Captain Stevens realized Patrick had gone completely deaf. This had happened to many men that day. Most recovered their hearing eventually, as did Stevens.

The lieutenant found a burnt splinter from the *Trippe* hull, and a piece of broken sidewall. He wrote, as clearly as he could, the words: "Many are deaf. Hearing will return. Rest."

But, for Patrick Fitzpatrick, the world had now changed dramatically. He held out hope that over the next few days, like others around him, including Stevens, his own hearing would eventually recover.

But there would be no return to normalcy for Patrick Fitzpatrick, or his hearing.

His thoughts turned to home and his sons. But when would he be able to see them again, even if he could never hear them again?

At right – The author found this document in the official records of the Lake Erie Islands Historical Museum, Put-In-Bay, Ohio. It is proof positive, as attested to by U.S. Navy Master Commander Thomas Holdup Stevens, that Patrick Fitzpatrick did serve as Pilot on the U.S. **Trippe**, *under the command of Stevens, during the Battle of Lake Erie. It also attests to the loss of hearing that Fitzpatrick suffered during that battle. The letters states that many men on the* **Trippe**, *including Stevens himself, experienced complete or partial deafness during the battle, though many of them recovered within a few days or weeks.*

On March 31, 1828, U.S. Navy Master Commander Thomas Holdup Stevens wrote to U.S. Senator Richard M. Johnson about Fitzpatrick's case:

"I have rec'd your letter of the 17th inst. accompanied with the petition and documents in the case of Patrick Fitzpatrick, the Pilot of the U.S. Sloop *Trippe* under my command in the action of Lake Erie on the 10th of Sep'r, 1813. I have no hesitation in giving it as my opinion that this individual was not deaf previous to that action and that his deafness may have been caused by the heavy cannonading on that day, I can readily imagine, without being able positively to corroborate his assertion. I can only state the general fact that a great proportion of my crew complained of deafness after the conflict and I know in my own case that my hearing was not perfectly restored till some weeks after the action. From the good character of this man, I should therefore be disposed to give credence to the declaration in his affidavit as to this fact."

Chapter Five
THE AFTERMATH

It was just after 3:00 pm when the British fleet finally surrendered. All vessels were anchored. Sand was thrown on the decks to soak up the great amount of blood that was spilled. Quick repairs were made to each ship, near West Sister Island.

During this time, Perry wrote his famous message to William Henry Harrison. On the back of an old envelope, Perry penned:

> Dear General:
> We have met the enemy and they are ours.
> Two ships, two brigs, one schooner and one sloop.
> Yours with great respect and esteem,
> O.H. Perry

The Battle of Lake Erie was decisive, but there was so much more that still needed to be done.

American casualties in the battle were 27 dead and 96 wounded. British losses numbered 41 dead, 93 wounded, and 306 captured.

Perry called his ship captains together for a quick meeting. "We need to get these wounded men back to Presqu' Isle as quickly as possible. Our remaining

The Aftermath

ships will ferry troops to William Harrison's command at Detroit."

"Fitzpatrick!" he asked, "Will you lead us there?"

Despite his hearing loss, Patrick could tell that the commander of the fleet was addressing him. Smithy helped him understand by writing some quick words on a piece of paper. "Do you think you can lead us to Detroit safely?" he asked.

For Patrick Fitzpatrick there was a lot at stake. His share of the $260,000 in prize money awarded to participants of the battle totaled $447.39. In today's money, that would exceed $5,000 – more money than he could make growing hay for the next few years to come.

Add to this the fact that he was promised an additional three months of military pay, plus a steady job, and Patrick decided, right then and there, that despite his condition, he was not about to say no to any request made by his superiors.

And then there was his pride.

He had always thought he could make the trip to Put-in-Bay blindfolded. Now he would prove he could continue on to Detroit with no ability to hear.

He answered, "Yes. Of course I can."

Colonel Smith and Lieutenant Stevens did their best to aid Fitzpatrick in his duties, in piloting one of the larger ships further west. Soon, they had enough hand signals to relay basic commands.

Patrick wasn't alone in his deafness, and so it was necessary that this type of quickly-invented sign language would be used for the rest of the men who were also hearing impaired.

Within days, the remaining ships, including the *Trippe*, began the journey back to Presqu' Isle with the wounded. Patrick led several other ships on to Detroit to fight alongside William Henry *Tippecanoe* Harrison, who later became the ninth U.S. President.

Over 2,500 troops had arrived to board the remaining American and former British ships for the trip west.

The lead pilot noticed, over just a few days, that he began hearing rumbling noises, which seemed to indicate that someone might be speaking to him. But he could not clearly make out the words. Between hand signals, and written instructions, he slowly learned to communicate at least with his closest friends and officers. "This will have to do, for now," he thought.

Upon reaching Presqu' Isle, the eastbound fleet of ships made their way into the bay, while the larger ships waited their turn to be cameled in over the bar. The *Trippe* was an exception.

Every British captain, and all the most experienced officers had either been killed or were seriously wounded. Barclay was no different. His limbs were shattered and part of his thigh had to eventually be cut away.

The Aftermath

Perry accepted Barclay's surrender with the condition that he would be returned to the British side, as was a common practice in many military campaigns. Perry chose the *Trippe* to make the journey to Buffalo, where Barclay would be exchanged for American prisoners. There, in December of that same year, Buffalo was burned almost completely to the ground by the British, in retaliation.

The *Trippe* became a victim of that attack.

However, Patrick Fitzpatrick was, by this point, in the small crossroads they called Detroit.

Most of the men who fought in the Lake Erie battle, including Commander Perry and Patrick Fitzpatrick, were sick with "lake fever" – most likely cholera caused by unclean water supplies. Patrick would have liked to have returned to Patrick's Run, but, due to fear of a more widespread epidemic, and the vast distance he'd need to cover during wartime, instead, he chose to write a letter to his eldest son:

Dear Hugh,

I hope that you and Lil' Patrick are well. I am not well myself, having acquired lake fever. Every one of us has been asked to remain until the sickness has passed.

I am sure you've heard aplenty of the battle we recently fought. Commander Perry is considered a great hero, but I'm here to tell you that there were many great heroes that day. We are now at Detroit in support of Major General William Henry Harrison.

We must continue this war until the British are run from our country once and for all. This is a great test for us. Can we survive as a nation unto our own? Can we stand up to the mightiest nations on earth?

Strangely, at fifty-five-years-old, I find myself now able to provide for you and Lil' Patrick in a way I have never been able to, in the past. You should soon receive a courier's package with a bank note for $447.39 in prize money. Keep it. I am not in need of it, as most of my needs are met, and I also receive a monthly wage. Please use this money wisely. I will return to the farm as soon as this war is over.

Your father,
P. Fitzpatrick
PS: I am deaf.

Shortly after the arrival in Detroit, Harrison's men, with Patrick serving in the line, chased the British General Henry Proctor, and the warrior chief Tecumseh, up through western Ontario to the Thames River, where they were finally defeated on October 5, 1813.

This American victory led to the re-establishment of U.S. control over the northwest frontier.

Apart from skirmishes (such as the Battle of Longwoods) between raiding parties or other detachments, and an American mounted raid near the

The Aftermath

end of 1814, which resulted in the Battle of Malcolm's Mills, the Detroit frontier remained comparatively quiet for the rest of the war.

The death of Tecumseh was a crushing blow to the Indian alliance he had created, and it was effectively dissolved, following the battle.

Shortly after the conflict, Harrison signed an armistice at Detroit with the chiefs or representatives of several tribes, although others fought on even after the end of the war.

The balance of 1813 was miserable at Detroit. Winter winds blew toward Lake Erie and Lake St. Clair at unbelievable speeds and many trees were blown down. Despite all the soldiers and sailors nearby, the world became a lonely place for Patrick.

The weather could blow incredibly hard from the north or northwest for a week or more straight, with the temperature dropping considerably.

Once in awhile, a southeast wind would bring unusually warmer weather for a day or so. This was always a welcomed relief for the men stationed at Detroit, and many chores and reorganizations were carried out during these respites.

Then the cold would set in again, and day after day the men prayed for spring, even if it meant going back to war.

Many left, come spring. However, the last of the British were not, as Patrick liked to put it, "run back home" until 1828. Patrick was in it for the long haul. He'd seen so much bloodshed and was being well-paid for his service, and so he thought it best to fulfill his patriotic duty until this war was considered completely over.

He continued to send money home occasionally for the use of Hugh and Lil' Patrick. He received a return letter every once in awhile, until the autumn of 1817, when everything changed once again for Patrick.

The Aftermath

At right – a woodcut of Oliver Hazard Perry, and his actual handwriting, written off West Sister Island, at 4:00 pm, on September 10, 1813.

We have met the enemy and they are ours: Two Ships, two Brigs one Schooner & one Sloop.

Yours, with great respect and esteem

O.H. Perry.

Chapter Six
THE NEWS ARRIVES

In early February 1817, a disaffected Canadian had made his way into the territory around Patrick's Run. He inquired about the well-being of the local citizens, and, along the way, he learned that Hugh Fitzpatrick was the holder of a considerable amount of money.

That autumn, Patrick Fitzpatrick received an envelope with a lengthy newspaper clipping inside.

It read:

On the 7th day of February, 1817, George Speth Van Holland murdered Hugh Fitzpatrick, an Irish Catholic, who, in 1810, settled about one mile northeast of the site of Patrick's Run. Van Holland first appeared in this vicinity at the cabin of Daniel Carlin, father-in-law of Mr. Fitzpatrick, and inquired how the settlers were provided with money.

Mrs. Carlin thoughtlessly said that her son-in-law, Mr. Fitzpatrick, had a greater amount than anyone near.

Thither the stranger bent his footsteps, the afternoon of February 6th, and requested permission to remain overnight. His request was willingly granted, and though the cabin contained but one room, he was nevertheless welcomed with all the generous hospitality characteristic of the Irish race.

The News Arrives

A bed was made for the guest upon the floor, and all retired to rest: but in the dead of the night Van Holland arose, found an axe, and sank it into the head of his sleeping host.

Mrs. Kathryn Fitzpatrick awoke, but fainted on beholding the horrible spectacle. When she recovered, the murderer demanded that she should procure the money and accompany him to Canada.

The fortitude and intelligence of the pioneer woman did not forsake her in the hour of trial. Apparently acceeding to his demands, she ascended to the loft overhead, poured her hoarded silver into a barrel of maple syrup, and returned with about $40 in bills, stating that this was all she had.

The inhuman monster now wished to kill her babe, which was only a few weeks old, but the entreaties of the mother saved its life.

He then ordered her to prepare the horses for the journey, and she went to the stable, turned out the animals and returned with the announcement that she could not catch them.

Van Holland then went to the stable and no sooner had he left the house than she seized her babe and her young nephew Patrick, darted out by the door, and hastened to the nearest neighbor, who lived some two miles distant. It was a bitter cold night, and deep snow covered the ground.

The murderer soon discovered her flight and started in pursuit, swearing vengeance on the wife of the victim. When he had almost overtaken her, the piercing wind blew out his lantern and he gave up the chase. The frightened woman sped onward through the freezing night, up the little ravine, and more dead than alive, finally reached the cabin of James Windors, in Erie County, Pennsylvania, to whom she told her tale of woe.

As soon as daylight appeared, the nearest settlers were notified of the crime, and on the following day, February 9, Andrew Britton, Baszilla Shreve, Bradley Winton and others found Van Holland encamped in the woods some three of four miles from the site of the murder. In May, 1817, he was tried, found guilty, and sentenced to hang.

From the date of his arrest until his execution he showed no sign of sorrow for his crime, or interest in his impending fate.

The crime for which Van Holland suffered death is without parallel in this portion of the state; and the only extenuating circumstance connected therewith, is the fact that he was believed by many to have been deranged, caused by a sunstroke received while serving in the English army.

~The End~

Patrick leaned back in his chair. He had read the newspaper article almost as if it had happened to someone else. But it finally sunk in that this was his own son who had been murdered. He'd seen so much death over the last three years, he was nearly immune to the thought of it. He'd seen so much hardship, and, of course, the loss of his hearing.

Now he had lost his son.

He cried.

Patrick was not one to cry. He was one to stand up to any situation, or any person – a fighting Irishman, if there ever was one.

But he could not fight the tears.

He wrote letter after letter, through the winter, addressed to his son's home near Patrick's Run, but never received a reply. In the spring he contemplated an attempt to make a trip back to Patrick's Run.

Then, about May of 1818, he received another newspaper article saying that his son's widow had married a well-to-do man named Patrick Coyle.

Coyle had adopted her baby, and her nephew Patrick, to be raised as his own, and he had promised to take good care of them all.

The article also stated that Hugh was buried next to his mother along Patrick's Run.

With this, Patrick wondered if he should leave well enough alone. He was gaining in years, and he knew he could never earn anywhere else what he was still getting from his military service.

In order to seek counsel, he went to speak with Father Gabriel Richard, who had built St. Anne's Catholic Church in Detroit, destroyed by fire in 1805.

"Father Gabriel," Patrick began. "I'm sorry to bother you on such a beautiful spring day with my problems."

"What is it Patrick?"

Patrick retrieved the two articles from inside his coat and held them out for the priest to read.

The holy man studied the documents closely. He asked, "This... this is the son Hugh of whom you have spoken so often? My dear Patrick, I am so sorry."

Though Patrick heard not much more than a mumble, he knew what Father Gabriel was saying. He simply nodded, "Yes."

The priest found a church bulletin and a quill pen.

He wrote:

"Dear Patrick. It is not enough to say that 'God has his ways,' or that 'We need to accept the will of God.' This is a terrible tragedy to befall you and your loved ones. It is something you will never recover from and it is something you will often cry over. However, you must accept what has happened, for there is nothing you can do about it. The Lord knows you have your own life to worry about. I will be by your side for whatever comes into your life. I urge you to forget the past, as best you can, and place your hope in God, and in your own future."

After allowing Patrick enough time to read the note, Father Gabriel Richard continued:

"We have both suffered loss. It has been a dozen years since my beautiful St. Anne's was burnt to the ground. Maybe we can help each other. Would you consider helping me build a new church, beginning next spring? Think about this, and pray on it."

Patrick did not need to pray on it, or even think about it. He'd been in the business of making war for so long. He'd stood in other men's blood on the decks of warships. He'd taken the life of other men who, like him, were just pawns in a game being played by the powerful. He'd lost his family because he was away at war. Finally, he was reaching an age where his skills in the military were not really needed and, for the first time in his life, he was actually facing the limits of his own mortality.

Maybe it was time to live a new, more spiritual life, for whatever days he had left on earth.

After all, Father Gabriel was a source of inspiration for all of Detroit. When St. Anne's burned in 1805, he wrote what became the motto of the City of Detroit – *Speramus meliora; resurget cineribus*; in English: "We hope for better things; it will arise from the ashes."

Perhaps now was the time for Patrick to rise from his own ashes. Besides, at the risk of his own life, Father Gabriel had supported the American cause in the recent war, and although he was taken prisoner, he refused to give up his allegiance to the United States. It was only through the efforts of an unlikely benefactor that he was saved from execution. The great chief Tecumseh, in spite of his hatred for the Americans, refused to fight for the British while Father Gabriel Richard was imprisoned.

Patrick, right there and then, pledged to help rebuild St. Anne's Church, to leave his military life as soon as he could, and to leave his regrets of the past behind.

The News Arrives

At right– This map is taken from the book **The Pictorial Field Book of the War of 1812**, *and shows Fort Detroit. The new St. Anne's Church, which was replaced again in the late 1800s, was located just outside Fort Detroit, where Patrick Fitzpatrick served in the military. Also shown is the Canadian town of Sandwich, which played an unfortunate role in the life and death of Patrick Fitzpatrick, and which later became Windsor, Ontario, Canada.*

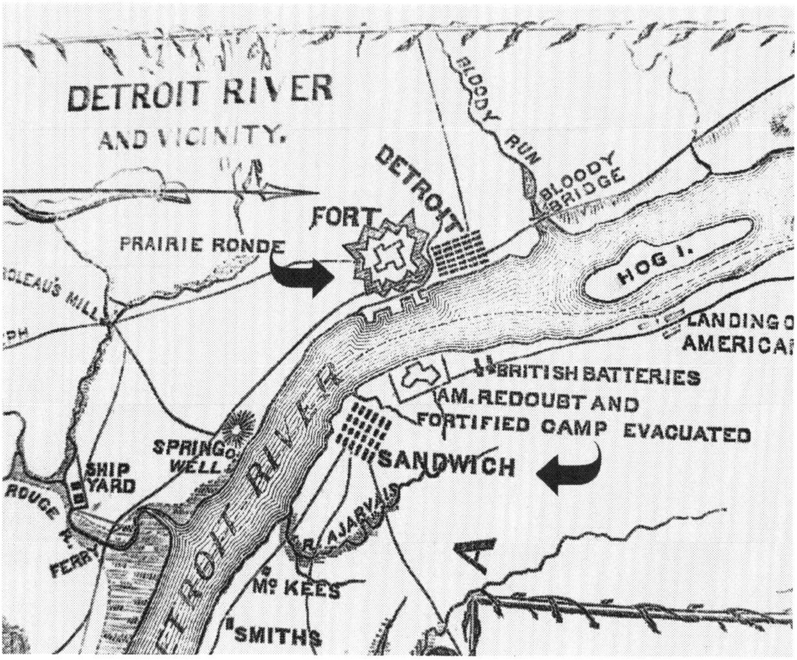
DETROIT RIVER
AND VICINITY.
DETROIT
BLOODY RUN
BLOODY BRIDGE
FORT
PRAIRIE RONDE
HOG I.
LANDING O
AMERICA
BRITISH BATTERIES
AM. REDOUBT AND
FORTIFIED CAMP EVACUATED
SANDWICH
SPRING WELL
SHIP YARD
ROUGE R.
FERRY
DETROIT RIVER
Mc KEES
SMITHS
A

Chapter Seven
A New Life

"Well, Patrick," wrote Father Gabriel, "We've waited for this day for a long time, but now here we are, ready to dig the first shovel full of dirt for the new St. Anne's Church. Will you please do the honors?"

Patrick, with shovel in hand, spoke to the assembled parishioners:

"Many of you know that I am deaf. Though I can't hear well, I hope I can speak for all the lost people of earth who have found their lives tossed and torn by those in power. In the words of our wonderful pastor, Father Gabriel Richard – 'We hope for better things.'"

With that, the old war hero lifted a load of Michigan soil and tossed it into a pile that, by day's end, would reach for the sky, if not *to* the sky.

Then he turned to Father Gabriel and said, "When you first find the time, Father, I need to speak to you."

The priest nodded in reply.

The day went well, and over the following weeks the church began to take shape. It was a welcomed sight for Catholics and Protestants alike.

Father Gabriel had been invited by Protestant worshipers to provide services to them as well, back in 1807, when they asked him to act as their clergyman.

Gabriel Richard owned the first printing press in Detroit and started *The Observer*, the Michigan Territory's first newspaper. He helped start the school that would become the University of Michigan, and he started primary schools for white children as well as for Native American children.

Father Gabriel Richard was even elected as a territorial representative to U.S. Congress. He helped initiate a road-building project that connected Detroit and Chicago, and worked for the improvement of conditions all across Detroit.

It was this never-say-die attitude that Patrick liked so much about Father Gabriel, and that made him decide to choose a new life at St. Anne's.

Later that first day, Patrick and Gabriel met for supper. "What is on your mind?" the priest indicated to his guest.

"Father. I am getting older every day. Soon I will need to leave the military life. Indeed, they have just kept me on because I am an old man – maybe an old war hero, but still an old man. If I do leave, I will need a place to live and money on which to live. I know that the church can only help me so much, and I want to stay here to see a new St. Anne's built. But I need to figure out a way to meet my rent and food expenses, at least. Beyond that, I don't need much. With my age and hearing loss, there are only so may jobs I can do, anyway."

Patrick wasn't sure what he expected Father Gabriel to say to this. He was simply looking for some type of inspirational advice.

The priest had brought some paper from his print shop with him to communicate with Patrick. He wrote: "As I understand it, your deafness was caused by your service in the Battle of Lake Erie."

Patrick nodded, "Yes."

"There must be some type of pension due to you for your injury, or even just for your service. Have you ever looked into this?" he wrote.

Patrick replied that he hadn't even thought about whether he'd qualify for a pension.

The priest continued, "I have some associates in the government and I will make some inquiries. In the meantime, don't worry about your meals, as you can eat here. What about your living quarters?"

Patrick explained that, until he officially left the service he would be allowed to stay at the barracks until he found suitable lodging.

"Good," Gabriel wrote, "At least you'll have a place to live, and can eat supper with me in exchange for your work on the church. I will look into any pension that might be due to you. And perhaps from these ashes will arise a new life. God bless you, Patrick Fitzpatrick."

It seemed a lifetime went by as Patrick worked each day on the new church, ate supper with his priest friend, returning to Fort Detroit each evening. There was not time for much else, and he was happy that someone as influential as Father Gabriel Richard was working to get him any pension that he might deserve. Day after day, he waited for news.

Every day became the same – work, eat, sleep, wait and hope – as he slowly let go of the tragic past.

The years passed. Despite Father Gabriel's efforts, Patrick had yet to receive any government help.

The work at St. Anne's was finished now, and the commander of the fort was anxious for Patrick to retire from the service, and to find another place to live.

Finally, Father Gabriel was able to get a letter from now "Master Commandant" Thomas Holdup Stevens, vouching for Patrick.

In January of 1828, Patrick took that letter to James Abbot, a justice of the peace in Detroit. He presented Abbot with a deposition about his service in the war, and his need for some type of assistance, especially if it was due to him by the government.

The actual words James Abbot wrote on that day were:

"January 31, 1828: Personally came before me Patrick Fitzpatrick, who deposeth and saith that he is at this time entering on his seventieth year of his age, being therefore old and infirm, and withal having lost his hearing in the memorable Battle of Lake Erie on the 10th of September 1813, this deponent in the month of August in said year lived a few miles back in the country from the town of Erie, in the State of

Pennsylvania, where he was at labor gathering the hay and harvest. It being understood by Commodore Perry that this deponent was an old sailor and well acquainted with the navigation of Lake Erie, and at the insistence of Col. Richard Smith, with whom this deponent had been for a long time acquainted, and who had recommended to the Commodore this deponent, that deponent accordingly volunteered as a pilot on board that fleet, that he entered on board of one of the light vessels on the second of September and piloted the fleet to the enemy, who fought, and were captured as aforesaid in which battle he lost his hearing and never since recovered it; that the certificate herewith annexed was given to him by the officer commanding the *Trippe* in the action, which entitled him to his prize money; that the deponent ever since that period lived by his labour; that being now so far advanced in age, he is unable to labour, his friends have advised him to apply for a pension."

The "certificate herewith annexed" was Stevens' first letter.

Later, on March 31, 1828, Stevens wrote another letter, which stated, "I have rec'd your letter of the 17th instant, accompanied with the petition and documents in the case of Patrick Fitzpatrick, the Pilot of the U.S. Sloop *Trippe* under my command in the action of Lake Erie on the 10th of Sep'r, 1813. I have no hesitation in giving it as my opinion that this individual was not deaf previous to that action, and that his deafness may have been caused by the heavy cannonading on that day, I can readily imagine..."

Now the wheels were turning, after so very long.

In 1829, Patrick began receiving an annual pension of $120, being paid out in $60 increments in mid-winter and mid-summer. He continued to live at the barracks, and to do odd jobs for the aging Father Gabriel. At least he was not destitute.

At least, now, he stood some chance of having a reasonably good final quarter to his life.

However, in 1832, Father Gabriel Richard passed away, scarring Patrick's heart once again.

Shortly before he died, the priest told Patrick that another, younger priest would soon be building a new church in Amherstburg, Ontario, Canada, and that he had highly recommended him as an honest laborer.

The younger priest was Father Angus MacDonell, and he would be the most important person in Patrick's life in the troubling days ahead.

One thing Patrick knew is that he missed Lake Erie very much.

He could not afford to move too far away from his friends in the Detroit area. Not being a river man, but rather a lake man, Patrick decided he would move to Amherstburg, still on the mouth of the Detroit River, but within sight of the waters of Lake Erie.

There he found lodging at Bullock's Tavern, owned by George Bullock. George would later build a much more famous Bullock's Tavern in Amherstburg.

The original Bullock's Tavern, however, was an old, two-story building Bullock had converted into a tavern and inn.

Father Angus MacDonell was holding services in a small chapel in Amherstburg, although a new lot had been purchased for a larger church.

MacDonell earlier served under Father Jean Baptiste Marchand, pastor of the Assumption Church in Sandwich Towne, Ontario, a town later to be known as Windsor, which was the seat of government for the territory that included Amherstburg. It was here where any major court trials would take place.

The new church at Amherstburg was named perhaps in honor of Father Jean Baptiste Marchand, but also through a special request by the bishop. The name of the parish church was to be St. John the Baptist's Church.

By 1830, it was obvious that a larger church building was needed, and government land on Brock Street was obtained in 1834. However, it wasn't until June 24, 1844 that the cornerstone was blessed and building began.

Patrick felt so blessed to now be a part of planning a second church. He helped clear the lot and eagerly drew up plans for the new church building, even if the actual construction was a long way off.

He and Father Angus got along well and soon Patrick became well-known among the local people.

However, his age was beginning to become a factor in how much work he could do.

A New Life

Between a little salary earned at the church and his yearly pension of $120, he was just able to get by.

From 1834 to 1837, Patrick continued to work as much as he could at the chapel, and at the new church building lot.

In 1837, with his income diminishing, Patrick decided to share his room at Bullock's Tavern with a maintenance man from the inn.

The man's name was Maurice Sellers.

Sellers was quite a disagreeable man. He drank whiskey heavily and he cursed worse than a sailor.

Luckily, Patrick was not able to hear the cursing, and so he quickly accepted Sellers as a roommate, thus cutting his room fee in half.

Patrick was fine with giving the bed to Sellers as he had always preferred sleeping on the floor, and had not been using the bed for much, anyway.

Patrick was himself known to curse and drink but nothing to the degree of Sellers. He noticed that he had to pick and choose his words carefully, when speaking to Father MacDonell.

At just one year away from turning 80-years-old, the hardened sailor, soldier, and laborer faced an uncertain future.

Day after day, he waited to hear news of when the building of the church would begin so that he could earn some extra money.

Day after day, his aches and pains grew.

And, day after day, he begrudgingly shared his living quarters with a man he came to despise.

Patrick wrote letters to random names he had heard of that now lived around Patrick's Run, hoping that somehow his younger son, who he lovingly called Lil' Patrick, would learn of his father and come to see him.

Patrick Fitzpatrick was living simply on hope, and not much else.

At right – This record from 1830 shows that Patrick Fitzpatrick received his pension money in two payments, once in mid-winter and once in mid-summer. It also shows that he was alive in 1830, contrary to some mistaken stories about his execution in 1828. He is listed first as "Patrick Fitzpatrick, late pilot," but this does not mean late in the sense that he was deceased. This is proven by the April 27 entry for ——— Sanders, who is listed as "late lieutenant, deceased." If Patrick were deceased at this point, the record would have said so. This is also proven by the second entry which lists Patrick simply as "Patrick Fitzpatrick, pensioner."

Patrick's Run

Date	No.	Name	Amount
Jan. 14	1,183	Richard R. Bradford, secretary	$27 17
Jan. 20	1,211	William Jones, postmaster	19 27
Feb. 18	1,313	John H. Maguire	56 00
Feb. 22	1,322	Patrick Fitzpatrick, late pilot	60 00
March 13	1,410	William Berry, late boatswain	600 00
March 17	1,436	John Goar, deceased	638 40
March 30	1,540	United States Branch Bank, Savannah	120 75
March 31	1,543	Henry Vickers, deceased	353 40
April 3	1,582	Jonas A. Stone, pensioner	80 10
April 12	1,640	Richard H. Bradford, secretary	62 50
April 17	1,664	Robert Spedden, late lieutenant	364 50
do	1,666	United States Branch Bank, Portsmouth	54 23
April 21	1,685	John Ball, boatswain	643 50
April 27	1,709	———— Sanders, late lieutenant, deceased	360 00
April 30	1,726	Branch of the Farmers' Bank of Delaware, at New Castle	48 00
May 27	1,890	Elizabeth Mays	57 00
June 2	1,923	Richard H. Bradford, secretary	41 78
June 9	1,948	United States Branch Bank, Baltimore	2,200 00
do	1,949	United States Branch Bank, Portland	500 00
do	1,950	United States Branch Bank, Charleston	400 00
do	1,951	United States Branch Bank, Lexington	550 00
do	1,952	United States Branch Bank, Norfolk	300 00
do	1,953	United States Branch Bank, Savannah	200 00
June 28	2,050	United States Branch Bank, Savannah	40 00
July 12	2,111	Richard R. Bradford, secretary	20 83
do	2,117	United States Branch Bank, Portsmouth	350 00
July 15	2,140	United States Branch Bank, Norfolk	600 00
Aug. 2	2,178	Patrick Fitzpatrick, pensioner	60 00
Aug. 7	2,215	George A. Rankin	25 00
Aug. 20	2,264	United States Branch Bank, Hartford	274 67
Sept. 9	2,332	William Goar, son of John Goar, pensioner	265 68
Sept. 10	2,337	Lydia A. Goar, daughter of John Goar, pensioner	835 68

Chapter Eight
THE CRIME

As Patrick made the trip each day from Bullock's Tavern to St. John's Church, he could almost feel his personality changing. At the inn he was the rough and tumble sea dog he'd been for a good share of his life. At St. John's he was the good church-going Catholic he'd also always been, whenever there was a church service available nearby.

He guessed that sinning every Saturday night and praying every Sunday morning had seemed to become the order of the day for a lot of people.

Being on the Cat, as he still called Lake Erie, seemed to be somewhere in between sinning and praying – more accurately, somewhere *beyond* it all.

It was spiritual, for sure, out on the open water, the wind wailing through the rigging, the slap of the sail.

The ghosts of those who had gone to its depths haunted him, too, if not as true apparitions, at least as memories of the stories he had heard about them.

Then there were the sunsets and sunrises. He missed the sunsets most. Sunrises were as common here, over the lake, as they were back at Presqu' Isle or Freeport, but the sunsets were just not the same.

The Crime

He thought back to the days of sitting on a rocky beach, on an old washed up log, with a big driftwood fire burning in front of him, and maybe a pint of whiskey, or a mug of beer conjured up in some neighbor's galvanized tub.

He remembered one such night when several of his friends were standing around the fire.

One by one, the men spoke of where they wanted to end up. One wanted to move to Washington, DC, someday to see the White House, maybe even run into the President himself.

Another wanted to keep moving west. He'd read in the newspapers about the journey of Lewis and Clark, and of all the wonders they wrote about.

Still another was satisfied to stay at Presqu' Isle to see how the little lake shore settlement would grow and prosper.

Patrick remained quiet all along. Finally, one of his mates asked, "What about you, Patrick? Where do you want to end up?"

After some thought, Patrick replied, "I don't want to 'end up' anywhere. I have no idea where life's gonna take me, but I hope to just enjoy the ride."

The closest he'd ever come to settling down was the year or so he'd spent on the Patrick's Run farm. If it wasn't for his military pay, he may not have even stayed in Detroit as long as he had. But now, life had taken him on an extraordinary journey.

"Some of it's magic, and some of it's tragic," he was fond of saying.

The rise of St. Anne's Church from its ashes had softened the blow, a little, of the loss of his family. The hope he found in the building of a new St. John the Baptist's Church again fueled his spirits.

Patrick's Run seemed like a lifetime ago.

Now, it was – "What can I do to help Father Angus? What can I do to make the balance of my life at least a little more comfortable? What can I learn from all I've been through?"

At times, Sellers would make a remark about a young lady, when Patrick was with him, and even though he couldn't hear the words, he would see the look of disgust on the woman's face and realize that he was being considered just as guilty, by association.

He considered his dealings with Sellers as a financial relationship only. The two roommates did not venture out into the streets of Amherstburg together, very often, or visit Detroit across the river, either.

He always had a suspicion that Sellers had his eye on Patrick's small pension. The sum of $120 in 1828 would be equal to about $1,500 in today's money, this being all Patrick had to live on besides the charity of Father Angus and St. John's Parish, coupled with his very inexpensive lodging.

Bullock's Tavern was shabby even by the waterfront standards of the day. There was always plenty of fish

The Crime

to eat, but there was a constant flow, in and out, of rough river men, lake men, soldiers on furlough or recently discharged, and old, often bitter patriots from either side of the War of 1812. It seemed like the word "nefarious" was coined just for this inn.

Beyond the clientele, the inn suffered, as do so many lake shore or riverside structures, from the natural molding process of damp wood. Movement of men, coughing incessantly, disturbed the hallways throughout most nights.

Add this to the smell of the public toilet room and the evenings would often find Patrick sitting outside on a bluff, within view of Lake Erie.

He sometimes thought what a pleasure it would be to smell a strong lake breeze again, or even draft horse manure at Patrick's Run – anything but moldy wood, dirty toilets, and the stench that seemed to surround drunken men.

Perhaps, as his pension continued, he might be able to save a little each year to eventually move to better quarters someday. Maybe even back to Patrick's Run.

On the night of March 2, 1837, Patrick was awakened by Sellers walking around the small room, apparently coughing, or drunk. His nostrils immediately filled with the smells he hated so much, and he decided he must get out of bed, as painful as that had become, and descend the staircase to the front door of the inn for a quick breath of fresh air.

As he passed an open door, he noticed the nine-year-old daughter of the inn's owner lying on the bed reading a book. "Mary Ann," Patrick asked, "What are you doing up so late?"

Knowing he was deaf, the young girl shrugged her shoulders. If he could have heard her, she would have told him that her parents had gone over to Monroe, Michigan to visit with friends.

"Aren't you too young to be up so late?"

Mary Ann shook her head no, then yes, then she shrugged again. She had no way of knowing how to communicate with Patrick, but she decided he was right and leaned over to shut off her light.

Patrick said good night and walked down the hallway to the stairs leading to his room, meeting Maurice Sellers coming out of the public toilet.

"That Mary Ann's a really fine girl," he said.

A few minutes went by, when Mary Ann heard a voice in the darkness. Her screams were muffled.

The next morning, Mrs. Quentin, nursemaid to the young Bullock girl, noticed that something was wrong, and she alerted the child's parents.

The sheriff and a doctor were called, and a medical examination was made, while the girl was questioned. The only thing the frightened girl remembered from the night before was Patrick Fitzpatrick's voice.

Mary Ann was known to be an exceedingly intelligent child, but then Patrick Fitzpatrick was

The Crime

known, by George Bullock, to be a sober, reputable man. It was hard to believe he could be responsible for an attack on Bullock's daughter.

Just then, Maurice Sellers arrived on the scene.

"I don't know who could have done this," Sellers chimed in.

"Or why," he continued. "She is such a young girl full of promise. And who would have even known where she was last night?"

He somehow discovered Patrick's knife in the bed coverings and, as if it had just struck him, he cried out, "Patrick! Patrick Fitzpatrick! Why that son-of-a-12-pounder-gun. I'll kill him."

The sheriff restrained Sellers to prevent him from going to his room to confront Patrick, but also to ask why he suspected that he might be the attacker.

Sellers relayed how he'd seen Patrick coming from the direction of the girl's room during the early morning hours, and remembered his comments about Mary Ann.

Earlier, Patrick had descended the steps of the inn to make his way to the daily ferry that would take him to Sandwich. Father Angus was sending him with a note to be delivered to the Assumption Church, in hopes that money would soon be forthcoming for the building of St. John's.

He passed the room where Mrs. Quentin was first tending to Mary Ann, as if nothing was amiss.

After checking at St. John's, where Patrick was so often found, Bullock made his way to Sandwich, with Maurice Sellers and a couple of deputies in tow. On March 4th, he joined up with Sheriff William Hands, a no-nonsense law enforcement officer, to find Patrick.

Together, these men made their way to the Assumption Church in time to see Patrick walking quickly towards the waterfront.

Sheriff Hands yelled to him, "Mr. Fitzpatrick. Mr Fitzpatrick. Stop! I want to speak with you."

But the deaf old man, unaware anyone was even addressing him, and in a hurry to catch the next ride down river, continued at a fast pace to the water's edge. The sheriff turned to his men, "Get him! Get him before he gets away! He's our man!"

Patrick felt the blow from behind. It was unexpected and it did its job well. He remembered seeing a bright white light for just a second or so.

The next he knew, he was in shackles and lying on the riverfront pathway.

Around him were several people, including the sheriff and Mr. Bullock. Patrick spoke in broken sentences, still in shock from what he saw, and felt happening to him. "What is...? Why are you...? Why is everyone looking so angry at me?"

Sheriff Hands, unaware at the moment that Patrick was deaf, fired off question after question, with no answers.

The Crime

Finally, he resorted to slapping Patrick in the face to solicit an answer; maybe even a confession.

Patrick screamed out, "Father Angus. Someone please find Father Angus."

Patrick was taken back to the inn at Amherstburg. He was led to the little girl's room, and was made to understand all that had just happened to him. She recoiled at the sight of him. Patrick slumped to his knees. He'd spoken to this young girl not so long ago. Now, she laid motionless, in a state of shock, with a nursemaid by her side.

The questions continued unheard by Patrick, but the scene that he now witnessed told him all he needed to know. "If you think I did this, you are wrong, Sir," he protested.

The sheriff replied, "Yeah, that's what they all say. You're coming with me."

Sheriff Hands was an enthusiastic lawmen. He rode around on a large white horse, making him very conspicuous to the town folk. Hands looked Patrick in the eyes and said, "We have a law here that says that murderers, rapists and horse thieves are to be hanged in a public thoroughfare with their remains in full view until the flesh rots from their bones."

Patrick wasn't sure of his words, but the actions of the lawman left no doubt as to his intentions.

Outside, awaited a paddy wagon with anxious looking horses pawing at the ground. Patrick was thrown, unceremoniously, into the back end of the vehicle. The hard landing hurt his aging joints, and the ride to the jailhouse back in Sandwich only made matters worse. By the time the lawman arrived at the home of the justice of the peace with his suspect, Patrick was severely bruised and further disoriented.

The suspect was led into a room at a farmhouse located at the corner of Dougall Avenue and Tecumseh Road. "Father Angus," he continued to cry out, "Father Angus. Will someone please get Father Angus."

Patrick now stood before a man in a judge's robe that just barely hid his farming clothes underneath.

"Mr. Patrick Fitzpatrick, you are charged with the molestation of the young girl Mary Ann Bullock, she being under the age of ten, which is a capital offense. How do you plead?"

Patrick struggled to understand the situation. Then he realized that no one there knew he was deaf.

"I can't hear you."

"Don't get smart with me," the judge retorted. "I'll see you hanged by morning if you don't cooperate."

Patrick continued his interrupted sentence, "I can't hear you because I am deaf. Please, someone find Father Angus, and tell him of my trouble."

The judge turned to the sheriff, "Throw him in jail and somebody go get Father Angus. We need to find out what is going on, and I have chores to do."

At right – A typical style inn from the early 1800s. Patrick's room was likely on the top floor, with a tavern and entryway on the bottom floor. Just across the cobblestone road was the mouth of the Detroit River, and perhaps a limited view of Lake Erie.

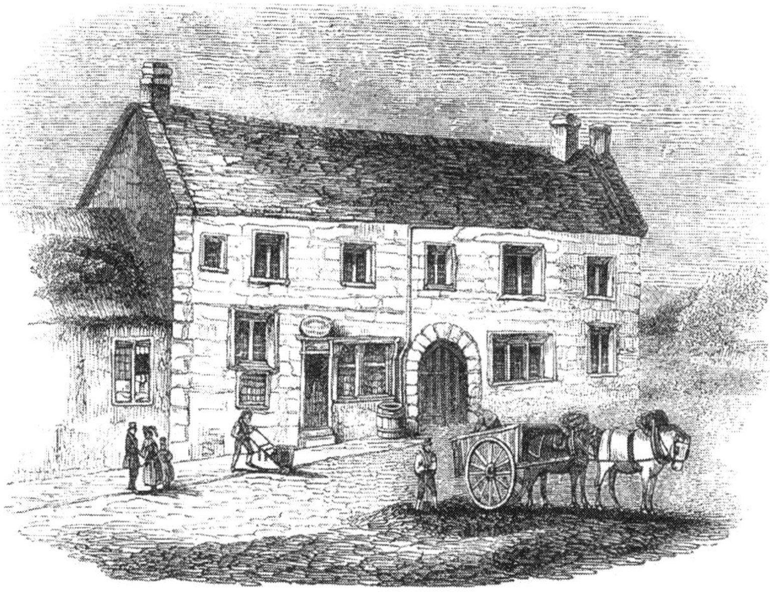

Chapter Nine
THE TRIAL

Local court cases at Sandwich Towne, and indeed all town hall issues, were handled at the farm of James Dougall. It was here that Patrick had his preliminary hearing.

Hangings, on the other hand, took place at the brow of the hill near Mill Street and East Russell Street. Sheriff Hands' jail was nearby. The original prison was in an old block house moved from Chatham to Sandwich, which was converted into the first jail for that town, until a new one could be built.

By 1820, however, a new brick courthouse with a jail was built at Sandwich. The Western District Commission of Oyer and Terminal, Court of Assizes would soon be in session at this location during the time of Patrick's trial.

If enough evidence was collected, Patrick would be taken in front of this larger court.

Patrick sat on a cot in his cell for days.

The sheriff was not interested in his story.

There was still a lot of animosity between the United States and Canada, especially at Sandwich, settled by a lot of former Detroit loyalists. In fact,

The Trial

American troops were still, just recently, working to oust the last British troops from American soil.

Having an American charged with such a terrible crime, and having a potential hanging in the offing, Sheriff William Hands may have seen an opportunity to enhance his reputation lying just ahead.

After a short while, Father Angus MacDonell came to the sheriff's office to see Patrick.

MacDonell handed the prisoner a note which read: "Patrick. Please tell me what you know of the assault on little Mary Ann Bullock."

After reading the note, Patrick replied, "I honestly know nothing of it. It is true that I saw Mary Ann reading in the very early hours of that day. I spoke to her briefly. But that is all I know."

Father Angus wrote, "Is there anything else you can remember? Can your roommate vouch for your whereabouts?"

Patrick replied, "Mr. Sellers was at the public toilet at the time. I saw him in the hallway."

Angus wrote, "And where did you go after you spoke to the girl?"

"I went directly to bed, and to sleep. I was heading to Sandwich with your note for St. John's the following day, and needed my sleep."

Then he added, "Father. I am innocent."

"I believe you. The question is – will the judge and the jury believe you?" wrote the priest.

Soon came summer, when Father Angus visited Patrick Fitzpatrick in jail, bringing with him a man of about 30 years of age. Holding Patrick's arm to steady him, the priest handed him a note which read, "Patrick Fitzpatrick, I'd like you to meet Patrick Fitzpatrick."

The prisoner was confused and stunned.

He looked up, and then he saw it. He saw his wife Mary's face. He saw the face of his son Hugh. And he realized he was looking at the face of his own son, Lil' Patrick Fitzpatrick.

There was nothing the elder Patrick could do but break down and cry. Then he looked again to make sure it was real. Slowly, he raised his tired body from the prison cot and reached out to awkwardly hug his son.

The two stood there embracing for what seemed like a very long time.

Father Angus said, "I am going to leave the two of you alone for awhile," as he handed the younger Patrick a small pile of paper, and a quill pen.

The two Patricks sat for the next several hours, the son writing his questions and answers down for the father to read. Many times, one or the other would begin to cry, and they both fought to hold back tears the entire time.

The elder Patrick told his son that he must apply for the old sailor's past, overdue pension, which had been halted upon his arrest. It was his understanding that this pension would revert to his heirs upon his death, which seemed more imminent than ever.

The younger Patrick said he would do just that, and that he would visit his father every day in prison.

And every day, the father would profess his innocence to his son.

The hours turned into days. Father and son spoke about many details of each other's lives. The elder Patrick learned that the creek on his old farm was still called Patrick's Run, although most people, now-a-days, left off the 's, referring to it as "Patrick Run."

It made the old man smile to think of that name again. It seemed that, now, "Patrick's Run" more aptly applied to the path that Patrick's life had run.

On September 17th, Patrick Fitzpatrick Jr. inquired about his father's back pay, (as shown by the document presented on page 109 of this book).

On September 20, 1837, Patrick was indicted by a grand jury, after a short hearing.

The jury trial started just a few days later.

The bailiff called on everyone to rise as four magistrates entered the room. This time their robes revealed the suits of a gentlemen beneath.

Off to the side were twelve jurors.

Also in the crowd, that day, was a young law clerk by the name of John Sandfield MacDonald. This man would go on to become the first prime minister of Ontario.

Despite the insistence of Patrick's innocence by his fellow clansman Angus MacDonell, John MacDonald felt that Patrick's guilt had been "clearly proven." He was of the opinion that justice was about to be done.

"Patrick Fitzpatrick, you are charged with the molestation of the innkeeper's daughter Mary Ann Bullock. How do you plead?"

Of course, Patrick could not hear any of the chief magistrate's words, but Father Angus had explained what would be taking place, and so he simply said, "Innocent."

"Who is the first witness?"

"I am," said Sheriff William Hands.

"All right, sheriff, what do you have to say?"

"I say that this vile man has practiced indescribable acts on a poor, innocent child."

"Yes, Hands," the judge answered, "But what is your evidence?"

"My evidence is that Mr. Sellers told me he saw Fitzpatrick in the hallway around the time the assault took place, and that Fitzpatrick commented on how Mary Ann was a 'fine girl.' My evidence is that, when confronted, the suspect ran until he was knocked down by one of my deputies. My evidence is that a knife belonging to Mr. Fitzpatrick was found in the room amongst the bed coverings, by Mr. Sellers. My evidence is that he has consistently refused to answer any of my questions over all of these months."

The Trial

"Your Honor!" Father Angus protested, "Your Honor, Mr. Fitzpatrick is deaf. He cannot answer the sheriff's questions unless they are written down."

"Objection overruled! Sheriff Hands, do you have any further remarks?"

"Just that this man needs to be gibbeted and hanged facing the river so that all Americans will see that they cannot come to Sandwich to further harass and kill Canadians."

"If that is all, you may step down. Are there any more witnesses?"

Mr. Sellers shyly raised his hand.

"Maurice Sellers. Come to the stand, swear on the Bible, and give us your testimony."

Sellers quickly placed his hand on the book and then took a seat next to the judge's table. "I testify that I saw Patrick Fitzpatrick in the hallway of Bullock's Tavern about the time he molested the young girl, and that he made lewd comments about her being a 'fine girl,' and that I found his knife in the bed. I further testify that when Sheriff Hands tried to stop him, he ran along the waterfront attempting to escape."

"Mr. Sellers. Do you own a knife?"

"I do not, Sir, but Fitzpatrick does. He is a former military man and sailor. Wielding a knife has come natural to him for most of his life."

Patrick was stunned that Sellers was testifying against him. They had shared the same room for several months, and although he disliked Sellers, they had never argued.

Even though they had not been close friends, he thought that his roommate should have known him well enough to know he would not commit such a horrible crime.

As the witness returned to his seat, Patrick looked him in the eyes and asked, "Sellers. Why?"

"Father Angus. Do you have any witnesses?"

"Well, Your Honor, we had hoped to call Mr. Sellers, but we see now that he is a witness for the prosecution, instead. I do have one other witness. I call Father Gabriel Richard to the stand."

The sheriff stood up, "Your Honor. I object. Richard is not even alive!"

"Sit down, sheriff. Perhaps he can still testify, especially in a capital offense trial."

Father Angus presented to the court several notes to and about Patrick Fitzpatrick, written over many years. Among them was the letter of recommendation Father Gabriel Richard has sent to Father MacDonell.

It read – "Dear Father MacDonell: I have known Patrick Fitzpatrick for ten or more years. I know him to be a good man and a good Christian. He, in fact, helped me rebuild St. Anne's Church after our terrible fire of 1805. I can attest that there is nothing in this deaf saint that should cause you not to take him under your wing. Despite his age, he is a good and honest

The Trial

laborer, and will help you build your church, if ever that should be able to happen."

"But Father MacDonell. Do you have any direct knowledge of the assault, or even of Bullock's Tavern, or Mary Ann's family?"

"I know only that they are a wealthy family from Amherstburg, but I have never been to the inn, and I was not present the day of the assault to vouch for Patrick's actions, except to say that he has been deaf since I've known him, and he, no doubt, had no knowledge of what had transpired, or that Sheriff Hands was trying to arrest him for the crime. I submit, Your Honor, that when a man is deaf, he can miss a lot of what is happening around him."

Then Father Angus made one final plea to the court. "Your Honor," he began, "I beg you to take this investigation slowly, and to have mercy on this poor man's soul."

"The investigation is over, Father. This is the trial."

The judge dismissed Father Angus, who joined Patrick at the defense chairs.

Patrick, his eyes welling with tears, thanked the priest for his words, having been told ahead of time what his testimony would be.

The judge barked, "Now, are there any more witnesses?"

Patrick never heard those words, but he stood up to say, "Mr. Judge, err, Your Honor, may I testify?"

The judge rolled his eyes, but said, "Patrick Fitzpatrick will take the stand."

When Patrick didn't understand, the judge motioned to the prisoner to come sit in the witness chair. Patrick stopped long enough to swear to the truth on the Bible, just to remove any doubt about his testimony.

"Your Honor, I am innocent. I know nothing of this crime. I don't know why Mr. Sellers would testify against me. I never knew anything bad had taken place at Bullock's Tavern, and I never heard the sheriff speak to me at the time of my arrest. I am simply an old, deaf man, living a life of poverty and faith. I am innocent."

"Anything else? If not, you may be seated."

The judge than motioned for Patrick to return to his seat.

"Any more witnesses?"

The younger Patrick raised his hand. "Sir, I do not have a testimony as I have only recently arrived in this province. However, I plead with the court to have mercy on my father – a father I have only recently come to know."

"If you have no pertinent testimony," the magistrate replied," then please be seated."

The silence that followed led the chief magistrate to declare, "This trial is concluded. Sheriff Hands, you will conduct the prisoner to his cell until a verdict is reached."

The Trial

Father Angus joined Patrick in his cell. Sitting with him on the bed, the priest wrote, "Patrick, whether you committed this crime or not, I think we must all agree that you may still may suffer the consequences. And for this you must prepare."

"But Father, I am innocent. I swear. I saw the girl. I talked to her. But I did not assault her."

Father Angus added to the paper, "If the magistrates should choose to find you guilty, we will appeal, and we will beg for mercy on your soul. There is not another recourse at the moment."

"But I AM INNOCENT!"

"Yes, I know. We know. Our Lord was innocent, too," the priest wrote.

Somehow, Patrick could find no reassurance in this statement.

After saying several prayers, and leaving Patrick with a Bible, the priest returned home.

The sheriff came to the cell bars and looked down on Patrick. "With any luck, this will be over by day's end."

Nothing happened by day's end. There was no word. Both Patrick and the sheriff were filled with the anxiety that often fills the hearts of those waiting to hear a verdict.

The magistrates, on the other hand, had a very serious situation to consider, and a decision that could be very significant and political.

If they ruled for the defendant, their fellow Canadians might be very unhappy. If they ruled for the prosecution, the City of Detroit, just across the river, might even take up arms to rescue Fitzpatrick.

Tensions were still high between these countries, and many arguments were still settled with violence.

The following day, on September 23, 1837, Patrick Fitzpatrick was informed of a guilty verdict and was sentenced to death. The sentence was to be carried out on October 9, 1837, at noon.

Immediately, a petition was started to ask for clemency for Patrick. The number of people who signed it was staggering. Among the signatures were those of eleven of the grand jurymen who had indicted him. Among the signatures were those of two of the jurymen who had found him guilty at his trial. Among the signatures were even those of Sheriff Hands and one of the magistrates that had led the proceedings. Numerous other people throughout the region, who knew Patrick well, also signed onto the petition.

The petition was taken to Sir Francis Head, Lieutenant Governor of the Province of Upper Canada, at Toronto.

On October 3, 1837, the Lieutenant Governor and his Executive Council denied clemency in the matter of *The Queen vs. Patrick Fitzpatrick*, and the sentence was carried out six days later, at the appointed time.

The Trial

*At right – This unfortunately very fuzzy-looking copy of an official government document was discovered at the Lake Erie Islands Historical Museum, Put-In-Bay, Ohio, and was closely studied. As noted on the document, in overlaid type: it refers to Patrick Fitzpatrick; it states that he was a Pilot on the **Trippe**; it states that he died in 1837; and it shows that an heir made a request for his pension on, or probably sometime just before September 17, 1837.*

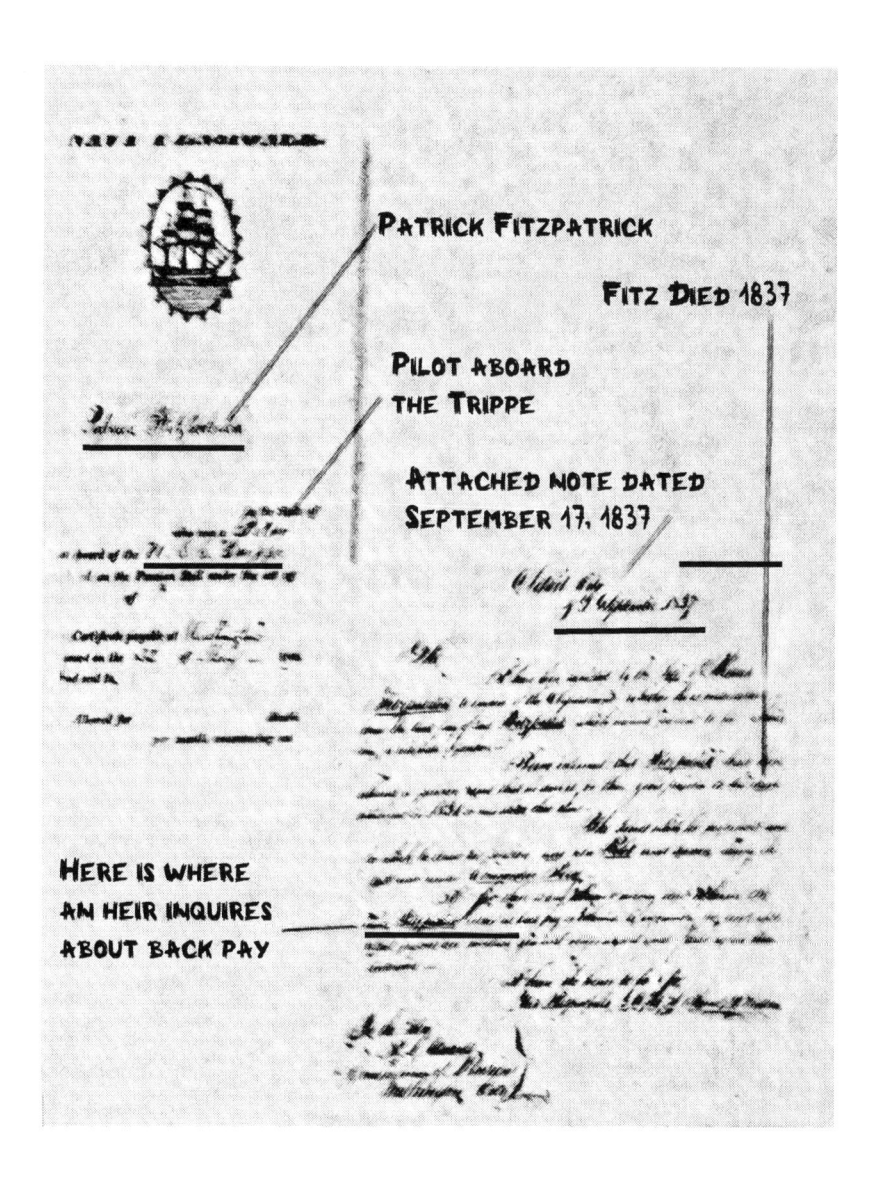

PATRICK FITZPATRICK

FITZ DIED 1837

PILOT ABOARD THE TRIPPE

ATTACHED NOTE DATED SEPTEMBER 17, 1837

HERE IS WHERE AN HEIR INQUIRES ABOUT BACK PAY

Chapter Ten
THE EXECUTION

When reading the verdict, the chief magistrate said, "This jury has been charged with determining the guilt of this man. The horrible assault on this young girl named Mary Ann Bullock must be avenged. On this we can all agree. While there is limited evidence, it is true that Mr. Fitzpatrick was seen in the vicinity of the girl's room on the night of the murder. It is true that he owned a knife, which was found in the girl's room. It is also true that, when first confronted by Sheriff Hands, he chose to run rather than answer questions. In the absence of any other evidence, it is, therefore, the opinion of this court that Mr. Patrick Fitzpatrick should be found guilty as charged."

The courtroom erupted with loud voices.

The magistrate called for order and proclaimed, "The defendant, Patrick Fitzpatrick, a resident of Bullock's Tavern, will suffer for his crime by being hanged by the neck at the hill near Mill and East Russell Streets. Execution to take place no later than October 9th."

"Your Honor." Father Angus insisted, "We intend to appeal this verdict. You must allow time for this."

The Execution

Perhaps to ease his own conscience, the judge replied, "Yes. You are correct. The defendant deserves the right to appeal."

"But, Your Honor," Sheriff Hands protested, "He is guilty. He must pay for his crime."

"Pay for it he will," replied the judge, "as soon as his appeal is heard."

It didn't take long for news of the guilty verdict to reach Patrick's old home of Detroit. Objections were made by the U.S. Navy, under whom Patrick had formally served. His friends also joined in on the resistance, and many signed the clemency petition even though they had no legal standing in Canada. Even the sheriff had a change of heart.

But now it was too late.

The site of the trial was directly across the river from Detroit.

Constant travel back and forth for social and business interaction only served to spread the word about the sad fate awaiting the lonely old Lake Erie sailor.

Like the trial, the site of the execution would also be directly across the river from Detroit.

Sheriff Hands reached for the billets of metal to constrict Patrick's movement on the scaffold.

"I guess we probably won't be needing these," he said.

Father Angus prayed incessantly from the Bible.

Lil' Patrick held his father's hand.

"Patrick," his father said. "When I am gone will you please return my body to Patrick's Run to be buried next to your mother, and your brother Hugh?"

"Yes," was the only answer Lil' Patrick could muster through his tears.

Indeed, in the valley of "Patrick Run" was once found a small grave marker with the single word "Fitzpatrick" carved on it – a memorial to this family.

Outside the crowd grew. Often, the community would turn out in celebration whenever a criminal was being executed. This time was different. The vast majority of the people did not want this to happen.

This time, the rush to judgement, along with the indifference of the Lieutenant Governor, was about to lead to the wrongful execution of an innocent man.

There was nothing anyone could do.

The scaffold was in plain view of the people amassed on the other side of the Detroit River. Several of Patrick's fellow sailors and soldiers were given permission to come to the Canadian side to say their good bye.

As Patrick exited the jail, the entourage from Fort Detroit stood at attention, arms in salute towards their brave comrade.

With Lil' Patrick at one arm, and Father Angus at the other, Patrick Fitzpatrick walked slowly towards the gallows to meet his fate.

An executioner in a hood waited at the top of the stairs.

"God bless, you father."

"God bless you, son."

"God bless you both," added Father Angus.

Everything seemed to be happening in slow motion. The crowd was in some cases cheering, and in other cases, protesting the sentence.

But Patrick could hear none of it. He was alone in his mind. Visions of the Cat ran through his mind. Sounds of the great battle roared in his ears.

Reaching the top platform, Patrick Fitzpatrick turned to the crowd. He spoke:

"Today, an innocent man is hanged from these gallows. The course that Patrick Fitzpatrick's life has run will soon be not much more than unimportant history. But, how many others, like me, languish in prison waiting to hear the trap fall for a crime they did not commit? I urge everyone who is here today, or who learns of this execution, to work for true justice in Canada, in America, and throughout the world. May my death, here today, serve as an inspiration to fight hard for accurate and fair justice for all people. And, may everyone always remember Patrick's Run."

Lil' Patrick Fitzpatrick claimed the body after all official papers were duly filled out. He loaded his father's corpse on a wagon to the sound of many people offering their condolences, and others their disdain. Lil' Patrick couldn't let it bother him as he had a long trip to make by wagon, and a lot of thinking to do about his father, and about his own future.

Several months after the execution, Maurice Sellers, roommate of Patrick Fitzpatrick, admitted, on his deathbed, that it was he who had molested Mary Ann Bullock, thus confirming the fact that Fitzpatrick was, indeed, innocent, all along.

Upon reaching the creek that bore his own name, Lil' Patrick buried his father next to his brother and his mother, and said good-bye, once and for all, to the old farm.

He decided that, once the burial was over, he would move a few counties to the east, into New York State, to marry a girl he had met there, and to try to forget everything there was to forget about Patrick's Run.

Everyone else seemed to forget, too, until clues began popping up, here and there, in 2012, just one year before the 200th anniversary of the Battle of Lake Erie, and began staring this author in the face.

The Execution

At right – This field, located near Spartansburg, PA, just south of Route 77, on "old" route 77, is where the Fitzpatrick gravestone was found. In early descriptions, the grave was said to be under a tree and marked by a stone bearing the Fitzpatrick name. The tree and stone are gone, but a recent owner of the property reported that a rectangular shape of clay was visible in the area where he had been told that the gravestone was located.

Patrick's Run

Chapter Eleven
THE RESPONSE

The State of Michigan startled the world, in 1846, by becoming the first English-speaking territory in history to abolish capital punishment.

This movement grew out of two incidents, which happened seven years apart, but whose effect was cumulative.

The first event was the hanging of Stephen Simmons in Detroit, in 1830. The second was the hanging of Patrick Fitzpatrick, a former Detroit resident, which took place in Sandwich (Windsor), Ontario, Canada, in 1837.

In the case of Fitzpatrick, people on both sides of the Detroit River were profoundly upset by this incident.

"Government," in the exercise of its judicial duty, coupled with a rush to judgement and an unconcerned Lieutenant Governor of Ontario, had put an innocent man to death; they had taken away something from this man that could not be restored, and put his family and friends through much despair and sadness.

And, they had also spit on the reputation of an American war hero.

Capital punishment soon became a common topic of conversation among the people of Michigan.

Surprisingly, in spite of Patrick's defense being handled by Father MacDonell, most clergy in Michigan were in favor of maintaining this type of punishment, citing the Bible verse of "an eye for an eye."

Others, however, were not so sure.

The Michigan State Legislature voted to abolish capital punishment on May 18, 1846, and this has remained the law ever since.

Although the death penalty was formally retained as the punishment for treason, until 1963, no person has ever been tried for treason against Michigan, and no person has ever been executed in Michigan since it became a state.

Before statehood, around a dozen people were executed in the Michigan Territory. Since statehood, only one man has been sentenced to death in Michigan under a federal government ruling, because his crime was committed on federal land.

Around the world, Patrick Fitzpatrick has become an inspiration for anti-death penalty groups, though often the wrong year of execution or the wrong crime for which he was charged are given.

Some say he was executed in 1828, and some in 1838, when court records prove it was October of 1837. Some say he was convicted of assault *and* murder, but it was strictly for assaulting a child under ten years of age, which was punishable by death in 1837. In this case, the child was just nine-years-old. Regardless, Patrick was innocent, as proven by the confession of Maurice Sellers to the crime.

Patrick Fitzpatrick appears on numerous web sites, although, until this book, his full story has never been told.

Though some of the daily details, in this book, have been fictionalized, the vast majority of important facts are supported by official military and government documents, uncovered and combined by the author, in order to tell a more complete tale of Patrick.

Information was collected from Museum Windsor, in Windsor, Canada (formerly Sandwich), from the Lake Erie Islands Historical Museum, at Put-In-Bay, Ohio, from the Erie Maritime Museum, in Erie, Pennsylvania, from a historian in Spartansburg, Pennsylvania, and from a historian serving as Captain of the Brig *Niagara*, at Erie, Pennsylvania.

In addition, regional history books and newspaper articles, along with several local records, international web sites, and the author's own personal knowledge of the Spartansburg/Patrick's Run area (and of life on Lake Erie) have all combined to allow him to paint a reasonably accurate story of this man.

Since 1973, 144 people on America's death row have been exonerated, most recently, in many cases, through the use of DNA evidence.

The Response

A study released in the *Proceedings of the National Academy of Sciences* estimates that one in every twenty-five people sentenced to death in America is actually innocent, representing about a 4% rate of innocence.

While it is easy to wish the worst punishment on someone convicted of a heinous crime like murder, it is also hard to imagine how we would react if we were just minding our own business, and were picked up one day for committing such a crime. What if we had our court case rushed though an imperfect legal system, and were sentenced to the death chamber, all the while professing our innocence?

This is the situation for so many people.

Since 1976, the first year for which records are available, roughly 1446 people have been executed, about one-third of those in the State of Texas.

Four percent of 1446 comes out to about 60 people who have suffered the same unbelievable and unfair fate as Patrick Fitzpatrick. And this is America!

Roughly 2,000 people per year are sentenced to death in foreign countries, each year, although it has been said that tens of thousands have actually been executed as political prisoners.

Just based on the 2,000 known executions each year, around the world, and using this as the average for every year since 1976, that translates as 80,000 people executed, with a projection of 3,200 of them possibly being innocent.

The author is not claiming that these figures are 100% accurate. But they are a rough guess based on information published in scientific journals.

The number could be much higher, but it is doubtful that it is much lower.

The death penalty, like other hot button items such as abortion and gun control, has its share of supporters and detractors. But, it is safe to say that if we were one of the unfortunate people to be wrongfully accused, we would most likely be against it.

At the very least, government needs to be thorough in its investigations, not rush to judgment, and not ignore potential evidence, whether it be circumstantial or anecdotal. After all, everyone is presumed innocent, until proven guilty, not the other way around.

There are lawyers working pro bono across America on questionable death sentence cases. DNA has been playing an increasing role in determining guilt or innocence during appeals. And all over the world, there are anti-death sentence groups, some with anti-death sentence web sites, many that feature Patrick Fitzpatrick as a sad example of runaway justice.

Patrick Fitzpatrick's story lay hidden mostly in military and legal documents, until this author retrieved them from the Lake Erie Islands Historical Museum, at Put-In-Bay, Ohio, Museum Windsor, in Windsor, Canada, and from other sources, to piece together the story of Patrick's Run.

At right – These images are actual "before and after" photos of a hanging in Sandwich, the town that eventually became Windsor, Canada. Who the victim is, in this case, is not yet known, but Patrick's execution pre-dated the common use of photography, so we know it wasn't him. As seen in the photo, it was the norm both here, and in most other towns, for large crowds to gather to witness an execution. Sometimes, a celebration was had, cheers were voiced as the deed took place, and a picnic might even be held. I suppose possibly the one person not enjoying himself would be the person with the rope around his neck.

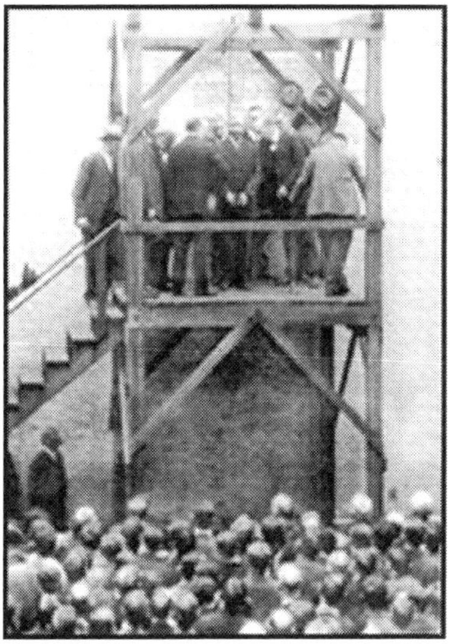

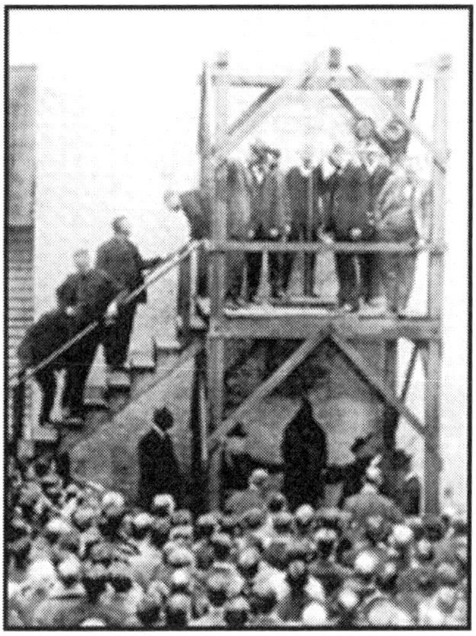

Epilogue

It is not the intention of this book to debate the merits of the death penalty, but rather to record the heroic life and tragic death of Patrick Fitzpatrick, an Irish-American war hero, before it was lost forever.

I thank those who have helped me in this effort:

- My wife, Beth McQuiston, for her proofreading and patience during the writing of this book;
- Pat Gustafson, Secretary of the Irish Cultural Society of Erie County, PA, for her proofreading and constant encouragement, over a four-year period;
- Constance Sitterley, Historian from Spartansburg, Pennsylvania, who provided old newspaper clippings and historical documents referring to both Patrick and Hugh Fitzpatrick, and to Patrick's Run.
- Captain Walter Rybka, who, while we were out sailing on the replica Flagship *Niagara*, told tales of the 1813 Battle of Lake Erie, and of early life on the lake.
- Heather Colautti, Registrar, Museum Windsor, for providing invaluable information about the criminal charges, trial, and execution of Patrick Fitzpatrick.
- And the staff of the Lake Erie Islands Historical Museum, Put-In-Bay, Ohio, for providing the military documents that were the genesis of this book.

~ The End ~

Made in the USA
Lexington, KY
06 June 2018